Blood Red Roses

Cenarth Fox

First published in 2025 by Fox Plays
Melbourne Australia

www.cenfoxbooks.com
www.foxplays.com

ISBN 978-0-949175-77-9
Cover design by Oliviaprodesign

Explanations

edhen - a person whose first and last names are of the same gender and are interchangeable, e.g. John Howard and Elizabeth Rose.

hened - (pronounced hen-ed), a person whose first and last names are of different genders and are interchangeable, e.g. Lily Andrew and Michael Grace.

The words *edhen* and *hened* come from the fingerprint pioneer Sir EDward HENry, an edhen and former head of the Metropolitan Police in London. The words are part of the five books in the series *The Schoolboy Sherlock Holmes*.

Anthony's Nose (Tony's schnoz) is an escarpment near Dromana on Victoria's Port Phillip Bay. Now much trimmed, today it's a popular boat ramp.

Probus Clubs

Rotary clubs are for people in business, to help one another and to support worthy causes. When members retire, they can join a Probus club designed for retirees. Members meet once a month, hear guest speakers and socialize. Trips and outings are offered to members.

Speaker Reviews

Cenarth Fox has spoken at more than one hundred Probus clubs, libraries, retirement villages, and literary societies on the topic of Sherlock Holmes.

We have only one question. When can you visit us again?
Patterson Lakes Probus
I would like to thank you so much for speaking to our Probus club. I've had many members say how much they enjoyed your talk with humour entwined. I've even had members ask for your website details, hence you can see you made a BIG impression with our members.
Middle Brighton Probus
Everyone who attended, loved it! Your charisma and wit had us all engrossed. The insight you provided on the well-known character Sherlock and his creator was engaging and interesting. The presentation was the right mix of humour and facts. We would have you back in a heartbeat.
Taylors Hill Retirement Village

Chapter 1
Sherlock and the Constables

Harry Penshurst loved the sound of his own voice. A bustling 70-year-old, real name Henry, Harry was the president of his local Probus club in Brighton, a fashionable and wealthy bayside Melbourne suburb. Always front and centre at monthly meetings, Harry ran the show. Here he was talking up future outings—not his job—and announcing birthdays of members for the coming month. Again, not his job.

Vice-president, Joan Wainwright, who doubled as the speaker co-ordinator, sat poised to introduce the guest speaker and died inside when Harry set off on the subject of today's talk.

'What is the matter with this man,' she groaned. *'It's my job to say all that. Perhaps if I shoot him, he might, only might, shut up.'*

Joan coughed, loudly for a refined lady, and a few members looked at her. Harry, selfish popinjay that he was, got the message—finally.

'Oh dear,' he said, 'I seem to have stolen Joanie's thunder.'

'Again,' said Joan under her breath.

'Come on, darling,'—God, he was sexist to boot,—'here's your mic.'

She stepped forward and accepted the microphone waiting for the president to get out of the way. She got him moving by starting to speak.

'Good morning, everyone. Today we have a speaker who has devoted his spare time to the study of the world's most famous fictional character, Sherlock Holmes. Cenarth tells me he's been a Sherlockian for many years and his talk comes highly recommended from many Probus clubs. As the great detective once said, "The game's afoot," so please give a warm Brighton welcome to Mr Cenarth Fox.' Everyone applauded.

1

The speaker was a tall gent with a full head of hair. Harry with his comb over disliked him from the off. The president loved having his photo taken but not when standing beside any male with an abundance of threadlike strands.

'Good morning,' said the speaker to which the members responded with warmth.

A slide appeared on the screen behind him. The words, *Truth is stranger than fiction* stared at the audience.

'Who can tell me who invented or is first recorded at having stated these words?' Silence. 'Guessing is allowed,' added the speaker and soon several possibilities were suggested.

'William Shakespeare.'

'Aristotle.'

'Albert Einstein.'

'Donald Trump.'

That last guess generated a hearty response.

'Thank you but alas the correct answer remains to be discovered. You'll have another chance a little later. But before that, let's begin with a quiz. I'll put the questions on the screen and please call out if you know or think you know the answers.' He paused. 'We could have a competition. How about Catholics versus Protestants?'

That produced barely a titter. The days of joking about another denomination seemed long gone. The days of most people going to church on a regular basis also seemed long gone. The speaker used to be C of E but was now more C *and* E—Christmas and Easter.

'Or Collingwood supporters versus everyone else.' That got the audience moving. 'Okay, let's settle for ladies versus gentlemen?'

The buzz increased and the questions appeared on the screen.

Name that Sleuth

Do you know your detective tales?

1. Simon Templar was known as ...
2. The religious detective was Father ...
3. Hercules Poirot originally came from ...
4. Inspector Morse's Sergeant's surname was ...
5. The magical sleuth in the windmill was ...

6. Dorothy Sayers created Lord ...
7. Sherlock Holmes retired to care for ...
8. The Baskerville pooch lived in the county of ...
9. Ruth Rendell used an Irish town for Inspector ...
10. Ian Rankin's Edinburgh sleuth is D.I. ...

'Okay,' said the speaker, 'Simon Templar was known as ...'

'The Saint,' cried a mix of male and female voices.

'The religious detective was Father ...'

'Brown,' many chorused. Probus club members are of an age when their knowledge is wide-ranging and often accurate. Many of the female members and a good sprinkling of the males were readers, some avid.

'Hercules Poirot originally came from ...'

'France,' called someone to be outshouted by others with, 'Belgium.'

The questions continued until number 8.

'Sherlock Holmes retired to care for ...'

Silence. Mutterings and whispers began until some brave soul called, 'Dr Watson.'

Laughter sounded but no-one knew the answer. The speaker continued. 'Mr Holmes became an apiarist, so the great detective retired to care for ...'

'Bees,' replied most of the audience.

Because the questions were on display, many members read ahead and cued their answers. The speaker looked to the screen and was set to ask a geographical question about the location of Sir Arthur Conan Doyle's most popular tale starring that painted pooch on the pasture.

But the question was never asked. A surprising and somewhat shocking event stopped proceedings as the main entrance doors to the meeting room opened and two visitors stepped inside. No knocking just a rocking in.

A man and a woman, well-dressed and far too young to join a Probus club, paused and looked at the speaker. He looked at them and was lost for words. Crime fiction was the topic but Mr Holmes, the detective who never lived so thus could never die, was busy in Sussex making honey. The interlopers introduced themselves via their attire. They were obviously from Victoria Police in the 21st century. The quiz ground to a halt. This was a first for everyone. The uniformed constables had never interrupted

3

a Probus club meeting before, and while the packed room heaved with fascinated members, no-one knew the correct etiquette.

Mr Spotlight, Harry, rose and strode to the front to take control.

'Good morning, officers. I'm Harry Penshurst, the president.'

He shook hands with the police then turned to the members. 'All right, let's be having you. Who parked in the street on the nature strip?'

Two members grinned but no-one laughed. Why are the police here?

'This is not a parking matter, sir,' said Constable Nicholas Bruce, an edhen. His female partner, Constable Brittany John, a hened, remained stony-faced.

'Perhaps you want the bowling club next door, officers. Quite a few shady characters in there,' said Harry working on his standup routine.

He grinned—alone. The president's comedy career never left the mounting yard. The silent room, now throbbing with rampant curiosity, gasped as the male constable detonated a grenade.

'Actually it's you we've come to see, sir.'

A pin fell to the polished wooden floor with its sound booming around the room.

'Me? About what?' snapped an indignant president. Then his demeanour did an instant one-eighty. 'Oh God, somebody's died? Who? It's not my uncle Claude? He's about to crack the ton and is expecting correspondence any day from Buck House.'

Constable Brittany John changed the mood. 'We know nothing of your relative, Mr Penshurst, and may we have a word in private?'

Harry gasped. The pressure gauge in the packed room fairly sprinted towards the red zone. Some members struggled to breathe. Talk about gripping stuff. What the hell is going on?

Margaret Penshurst, wife of the president, left her reserved aisle seat in the third row and joined the trio at the front. Her seat wasn't officially reserved but as First Lady in the Brighton Probus club, tradition and seniority demanded she be so seated.

'Henry, what's going on?'

As if Harry wasn't under enough pressure, now his busybody spouse picked up her megaphone and called the old boy by his given name. Harry hated the name Henry.

Constable Bruce opened the main door. 'This way, sir, if you please.'

Harry moved, Margaret followed and the quartet went to the foyer.

The speaker and his subject of Sherlock Holmes died a death. He stood before his audience imitating a shag on a rock. The buzz of conversation by members ruled the world. The most spoken comments were as follows.

'Why are the cops here?'

'What's Harry done?'

'Did you know his name is Henry?'

'Margaret looked ropeable.'

'I've always suspected he was a bit dodgy.'

Speaker co-ordinator and vice-president Joan stood and took the microphone from the chap wearing the deerstalker. She spoke quietly to him then turned to the still buzzing members.

'Come now, everyone, let's settle and give our speaker the attention he deserves.' The hubbub fizzled but their minds were elsewhere.

Mr Fox had never encountered a *lecture interruptus* before but given the nod, re-started his presentation. The slide on the screen changed and the speaker resumed his talk.

'Now let's see if we can match the first and second names of these famous detectives. We start with something dead easy. It's Sherlock ...'

Match the Sleuths

Sherlock	Spade
Dick	Chan
Perry	Holmes
Sam	Tracy
Nero	Marple
Jane	Rockford
Mike	Lupin
Jim	Wolfe
Charlie	Hammer
Arsene	Mason

Before everyone could respond with "Holmes," a raised voice outside the room brought the lecture to a halt—again.

'What!' shouted an irate president. 'There's a dead body buried in my garden!'

Inside, the hubbub exploded. For many, this was the best Probus meeting ever. Forget the speaker. Forget Sherlock Holmes. Our president is a killer. Hey, here's an idea. As a Sherlockian, could the speaker step in and crack the case?

Joan went to the speaker and chatted briefly. He smiled and began packing his equipment. The slide vanished from the screen and the speaker vanished from the building. A two-minute presentation was a first for him.

Outside in the corridor, Harry didn't manage the pressure well. The two cops were firm but fair. They let Harry vent his spleen.

'Will you kindly explain what this is all about? You drag me out of a public meeting, a Probus club, a legally constituted gathering with neither an "excuse me" or a "by your leave." Don't you know I'm the democratically elected president of this extremely popular club. We have a waiting list as long as my arm.' He gesticulated, something he did often.

The president took a breath and Constable John, the female officer, seized the moment. 'We'll be happy to explain, sir, if you'll stop speaking.'

'Yes, shut up, Harry,' ordered his spouse.

Two women giving Harry a dressing down only increased his rage but the placid behaviour of his visitors pushed him towards silence. Besides, curiosity hammered his brain. *What is this all about?*

'We have serious news, Mr Penshurst,' said the female constable.

'What?' demanded Harry. 'Is it to do with me or my wife?'

She took over. 'Don't be ridiculous, Harry and keep your voice down. Half of Bay Street can hear you.' She turned to the police. 'What's going on?'

'It's nothing,' snapped the president to his wife.

She kicked off. 'Nothing! Two police officers remove us from a meeting and it's nothing!'

Constable Nicholas Bruce, the edhen, took the lead. 'We apologize Mrs Penshurst. We're trying to explain although your husband keeps interrupting.'

'Yes, be quiet, Harry,' did the trick although he looked apoplectic.

The police stalled. They figured the locomotive would eventually run out of steam and come to a hissing stop. They were right.

The male constable paused then slipped into official speak boosting the tension. 'You are Henry Penshurst of 29 Buchanan Close, Brighton?'

Wow. This formal question made the situation seriously serious.

'Yes,' replied Harry now switching to a desperate voice. 'Please,' he begged, 'what's happened?'

'To put it bluntly, sir, we've found what we believe is part of a dead body buried in your back yard.'

Margaret flinched but Harry snapped.

'I haven't got a back yard; it's a rear garden.'

The police exchanged a subtle glance. This was not going to be easy.

Constable Bruce continued. 'We'd like you to accompany us to the police station, sir, to answer ....

Harry exploded. 'You're accusing me of murder and arresting me without reading my verandah rights. This is outrageous!' The president had been watching too many American TV detective shows. Unlike the United States, Australia doesn't have those so-called Miranda rights.

'Harry,' said his wife trying to stop his erratic outburst. She pointed to the now silent meeting room and whispered. 'Everyone can hear you!'

He settled a little. Constable John took over.

'You are not under arrest, sir. You are not being detained or charged. We simply wish to ask some questions about the human remains found on your property. Will you please accompany us to the station after which we will deliver you back to this venue?'

What could Harry say? He grunted.

'Although, sir, I should point out your property is now a crime scene and you and your wife will not be granted access to the rear until the police investigation is complete.'

'What!' demanded the president who now had a supporter.

'You can't do that,' fired back Margaret. 'I've got 6 dinner guests at 8.' She was confused. It was 8 dinner guests at 6.

It's fair to say, in the meeting room next door, the entertainment for this Probus club monthly meeting was rated at more than five stars. 5½★.

The constables struggled. 'Please, sir,' said Constable Bruce. 'There is no body just a limb. Apparently your dog started digging in your back yard and ...

'I tell you I haven't got a back yard; it's my rear garden,' fumed Harry who never grasped the meaning of *sotto voce*.

'Let him finish,' snapped Margaret sending her husband's blood pressure soaring. She was the only person who could speak like that to *il presidente* and get away with it. Constable Bruce continued.

'The gardener saw the dog digging and went to explore. He examined the object and thought it suspicious. He consulted the cleaning lady and together they decided to call the police.'

'They should have called *me*,' boomed the president.

'Shut up, Henry,' said Margaret and the police wondered if a case of mariticide was on the cards.

'We arrived at your property, saw the body part, and called forensics. They declared the limb to be human and a crime scene was established. We would like you and Mrs Penshurst to help with the investigation.'

Harry was off the bit. 'You're investigating me for murder!'

Margaret wanted to belt him. 'Oh Henry,' she wanted to say, 'Will you shut the **** up!' Sensibly, she settled for, 'Will you give it a rest!'

The police struggled. 'Mr Penshurst, you are not under arrest.'

Margaret headed back inside. 'I'll get my handbag.' She disappeared.

Constable John moved to open the front door. 'This way, please sir.'

Harry glowered. He looked like he'd backed a horse that ran stone cold motherless last in a maiden at the Nyah trots.

Inside, the buzzing stopped on a sixpence when Margaret appeared. Every eye homed in on the president's wife. She collected her bag then made an announcement. Why? The handbag was far too small for all her dirty linen. Leave it in there, woman! Make it a no-washing day. But no, the long-suffering spouse couldn't help herself. She may as well have grabbed the microphone.

'It's nothing, everyone. Archie jumped in the rose garden and dug up some old bone. The police reckon it's human so off to jail we go.' She headed back to the foyer stopping at the door. 'I'm furious because I've always told Henry to bury the bodies under the house.' She waved. 'Carry on, Joan.'

The door closed and the room exploded.

Chapter 2
"Bent by name and bent by nature"

Sir Thomas Bent (1838-1909) was an Aussie and knighted, although not a knight. He was also a frightening left-arm quick bowler sending down swinging yorkers in his younger days.

Multi-tasking was one of his strengths. When appointed Premier of Victoria, he also became the state treasurer and took on the portfolio for railways. Busy boy.

Shenanigans and dirty tricks were a part of Bent's routine. Male suffrage existed but only for gentlemen who were financial, a paid-up ratepayer. As the collector of rates, Bent would "forget" to collect the rates of his opponents thus denying them the vote on election day. Sneaky.

Tom started life in Sydney not long after Queen Victoria was crowned. He was the oldest of six little Bents and when his old man, a convict transported to the colonies, got into financial strife, the Bents left New South Wales for Victoria.

Trains and planes were not common in mid-19th century Australia so horse and cart and Shanks' pony got the Bents 500 miles south.

They moved to Melbourne and there it was Thomas Bent rose to the highest political rank in the state. When he died in 1909 he'd been any number of ministers, the speaker of the Legislative Assembly and the premier.

No posh school or university education for our Tommy. He got his hands dirty, literally, working for the old man in a market garden in Brighton. His three younger brothers got busy with the carrots and carnations as well. Brighton wasn't the upmarket suburb it was to become when Harry Penshurst made his mark there. Many of Brighton's finest residences today, including the one owned by Harry Penshurst, were once open fields with vegetables and flowers in abundance.

Tom was lucky or clever or both when he took an interest in local affairs. You'd think he'd put people off when he became the local rate collector. But Mr Bent had a way with words and knew how to make himself popular.

His political career began in a humble post when elected to the Moorabbin Roads Board in 1863. Hardly a prestigious international body but the young man rose within its ranks to become its chairperson. This type of move, winning promotion from within, would be repeated several more times in his career.

The House of Assembly is Victoria's lower house but the one where bills are generated and the Premier resides and in 1871, Tom was elected, to everyone's surprise, the Member for Brighton, and so off to Spring Street he went. Not bad for a bloke with a limited public education in working-class Fitzroy and a working life as a market gardener. Mind you, having worked for his old man, Tom later set up his own market garden in Brighton and didn't let the lettuce grow under his size 9s.

Now Melbourne, in the second half of the 19th century, was ripe for development. Land was available and once it was developed and houses appeared, the new residents needed services and one main service was public transport. Trains and trams were in demand.

Bent and politics went together like a pig and mud. He was a natural negotiator. He did the right thing by his locals which was much appreciated. Multi-tasking was a doddle for Tom who slipped into local councils with ease and became the Mayor of Brighton as well as the Member thereof in state parliament.

This gave him the opportunity to poke his nose into the development of land in and around his residence. He bought land in the area and subdivided it. He built houses on his own land and sold or rented them. He bought land using government money and at times without Cabinet approval. What he didn't know about progress in his and surrounding suburbs wasn't worth knowing. If people on council or in parliament objected, he slipped into his bully costume and got his way.

Our man speculated and snapped up land elsewhere. He bought property in the heart of Melbourne and sold it the same day for a whacking great profit. Within state parliament, his responsibilities grew when appointed the Commissioner of Railways. Bent talked up the octopus dream where the state was to have tentacles of railway lines snaking in all directions. A railway in every electorate? No wonder he got elected.

Trains and trams just happened to be built within cooee of land owned by Tommy Bent. Naturally, this increased the value of his properties. Was he challenged about this possible conflict of interest? Yes but he stood up to his critics, browbeating half a dozen to resign. Not until late in his career did any official investigation begin but by then his failing health took the wind out of his opponents' sails.

In the 1880s, Melbourne land prices boomed. Some prices matched those in London. But not all speculators were successful and some came unstuck. Tom survived and had what might be called a mid-life crisis. Forget politics, he became a cocky. He ran a dairy farm about two hundred miles south west of downtown Brighton near Port Fairy but continued his interest in both local (Melbourne) and state politics. Travelling to Melbourne for meetings was a massive trek but in 1900 he was again elected the Member for Brighton and back to state parliament he went.

As was the case before, Mr Bent refused to stand still. He became the Railways Minister and two years later was elected by his colleagues as the Premier of Victoria.

An investigation into his activities found he made no monetary gain although some of his moving and shaking was questionable, highly so.

He scored an impressive grave in Brighton and an even more impressive statue. The latter needed to be relocated due to road widening, a type of progress you reckon Tommy would have approved.

There was a time when the team which won the premiership in what was the local football competition, the VFL, would be acknowledged by some wit decorating Tommy's statue with the scarf and beanie in the colours of the winning team.

That move could be said to prove, however suspect he may have been, Tommy Bent was clearly a man of the people. Nobody gets a suburb named after them, Bentleigh, a street in several suburbs; there's a Bent Street in Bentleigh, Richmond, Kensington and West Melbourne, and a saying, "Bent by name and bent by nature."

Go Tommy!

Chapter 3
Three amateur sleuths

Joan asked the speaker to POQ (Pass out quietly) promising him a second gig soon, the rozzers escorted the Probus club King and Queen off the premises, and the 103 remaining members joined the gossipy bun fight. You could swim in the sea of wagging tongues.

Nobody stood to take control. Who could control this mob? Sisters Patricia, a tall spinster and Jean, a not so tall widow and mother, got rabbiting. 'Did Margaret say the bone was human?' asked Jean of Big Sis.

'Well the cops would hardly be here if it was one of Archie's forbears.'

'Let's ask the silent assassin,' said Jean. 'He'll know.'

Robert Ayres, the retired police officer member of the club, could have been called Still Waters. The former senior constable rarely spoke publicly when at Probus. But the sisters knew he was a deep thinker and one whose thoughts were worth hearing. Plus he spent 40 years in Victoria Police. The siblings called him, privately of course, Bobby Squared as in Bobby[2], i.e. Bobby the Bobby.

They found him seated towards the rear, his usual spot where he shunned the limelight. Right now he sat alone because people got up and moved after the recent bombshell events. The sisters approached from different directions. Patricia sat on his left and Jean his right.

'Good morning, Senior,' said Patricia.

He smiled. 'Good morning, ladies. And how are my favourite Probus sisters this fine day?'

'We're both well, sir. And how is your good lady?'

Robert's wife had been unwell of late and no longer attended meetings. But Probus meetings were his release valve. A neighbour or his daughter would arrive to sit with Mrs Ayres allowing Bobby the Bobby to leave the property for a couple of hours and enjoy the speaker and the company of fellow members.

'She's had a good month, thankfully.' The sisters purred. 'When the weather changes, Glenda always seems brighter.'

'Please give her our love,' said Jean and Robert nodded unable to say "Thank you" due to a lump giving birth in his throat. He found kindness moving and especially as the sisters were genuine. Plus living with someone who is dying puts a bit of starch in your underwear.

'Now officer,' said Patricia, 'we need your expert opinion. What do you make of the sudden arrival of the two gendarmes?'

Bobby was thrilled to be asked, to have his record of service acknowledged. 'I'm certain of one thing.' The sisters hung on his every word. 'It's true you know you're getting old when the police look so young.'

The sisters laughed, not that you could hear them with all the gossiping in the room.

Patricia pressed with a gentle touch. 'So have our suspicions finally been proven correct? Is our president a homicidal maniac?'

A wispy smile appeared on Bobby's lips. 'I'm perplexed as to the timing. I mean to get a forensics team to a murder scene is ...'

'So it *is* a murder,' gasped Jean.

Patricia shushed her sister. 'Jean!'

The rebuke hit home. 'Sorry, Officer, please continue,' said Jean.

Bobby was in his element. 'In my day, it might take hours to get the specialist to a crime scene and then testing for cause of death could be even longer, days, weeks on a tricky job. Here we have the dog finding the bone at say 0800 hours, the local constables attending at once, the quick forensic decision and the constables arriving here at 1114 hours. That's more like a scene in a detective series on TV or in a crime novel.'

The sisters were ecstatic and wanted more. 'But is it possible? asked Jean. 'Should we now be looking for a new president?'

'Anything's possible but it would all depend on the condition of the bone or body part.'

'Meaning?' asked both sisters in unison.

'Well if it's human and ancient, that tells us next to nothing and the likelihood of Harry being the butcher of Brighton is nigh on impossible, but if the remains are of a recent origin, then that may open a very large can of wriggling worms.'

'There'd probably be worms in the garden anyway,' offered Jean.

Patricia and Bobby looked at her, wondering if she was serious. If not, her pun was almost witty.

'What is happening to Harry and Margaret right now?' asked Patricia.

'General interview, have you seen anyone in the area acting suspiciously, how long have you employed your gardener, what do you know about him? Unless Harry breaks down and confesses to disposing of a body, I expect they'll both be back here within the hour.'

'In time for lunch,' added Jean. 'That'll be interesting. Are you coming, Bobby?'

She could have bitten her tongue. The retired cop always set off for home as soon as the monthly meeting ended. He was an unrecognised hero caring full-time for his wife.

Detective Inspector Charlotte Fairfax was appointed the SIO (Senior Investigating Officer) in the case which could be nothing or, possibly a cold case in waiting. At the police station she greeted the Penshursts, introduced herself and escorted them to an interview room, the sort offered to victims of crime. When all were seated, she produced her file and prepared to speak.

'Do I need a lawyer?' snapped Harry. Margaret groaned.

'No you don't, Mr Penshurst. Unless you murdered someone and buried a part of the body in your rose garden.'

'Should you be reading us our verandah rights?' Back in Arizona, poor old Ernesto Miranda spun in his grave.

The detective hid her smile. 'No sir because you are not under arrest or being questioned as a suspect. Please let me explain.'

'I wish you would,' said Harry, his frustration running hot.

'There was an incident on your property this morning which the police are investigating. No-one has been arrested and you and Mrs Penshurst are assumed to be entirely innocent. You may leave at any time and once this meeting is over, you will be driven home.'

'I don't want to go home. I'm the president of my local Probus club which has a membership as long as your arm with a waiting-list to match, and I need to return to my members.'

'Of course, sir, and the sooner we finish this interview; the sooner you can rejoin your meeting.' She paused. 'Now, may we continue?'

Margaret jumped in. 'Please do. I would like to know the details.'

'We both would,' added the president. 'What happened—exactly?'

The detective looked at her notes. 'The gardener saw your dog digging in the rose garden. The animal was restrained and the gardener saw what turned out to be part of a human arm, about three hundred millimetres or a foot in old money, or an old-fashioned cubit if you know your bible.'

Margaret's glare stopped Harry in his tracks. The DI continued.

'The gardener spoke with the cleaner, and the couple agreed they should call the police.'

'They should have called *me*,' snapped Harry.

Margaret was set to explode. Having been married to Henry Fitzgibbon Leigh Penshurst for decades was, according to many, both courageous and horrendous and worthy of a Bravery Medal. Harry became worse as he grew older and his wife had more than once searched online and at the local library for any tome, fiction or non-fiction, on *How to Bump Off Your Husband and Get Away With It*. Another appealing title being *Mariticide for Dummies*.

'Can you tell me,' asked the officer, 'if you've had a run-in with neighbours, people at your Probus club, anyone who might wish to harm or embarrass you?'

'I haven't an enemy in the world,' said Harry with feeling. Had he been attached to a polygraph when he gave that answer, the needle would have jolted as if making drunken contortions. Many people disliked Harry with a fair minority of them hating him.

'What about you, Mrs Penshurst? Can you think of anyone who might have placed that object in your garden?'

Margaret hesitated. 'No, but are you sure about it? I mean if it's from a dog someone buried years ago, what's the problem?'

'Exactly,' said Harry keen to depart.

'I wish it was an animal,' said Charlotte. 'The forensics team were certain it's from a human and not long deceased.'

'So where's the rest of the body and could the armless owner still be alive and kicking?' asked Harry. 'I mean if you've found a head or a heart, fair enough, but just because you've found a non-vital part of a body doesn't mean the person is dead.' He had a point.

The detective took a breath. 'The state of the arm would suggest otherwise. I should tell you your backyard is ...

'Rear garden,' snapped Harry. 'I don't have a backyard.'

'Your rear garden is currently sealed off as a crime scene.'

'Don't!' snapped Margaret and hubby, unusually for him, backed down.

'It won't be forever and you're free to access your home via the front. We've had a cadaver dog inspect your property, and it appears the remainder of the victim's body is elsewhere, certainly not on your land.'

'Wonderful,' sneered the sarcastic president.

The detective handed Harry a business card. 'Please, both of you, contact me at any time if you think of anyone or anything which may have caused or is connected to this incident. Naturally, I'll keep you informed of any progress we make.' She smiled. 'Now, is there anything you wish to say or question you wish to ask?'

She looked at two sullen faces. Harry couldn't help himself.

'Will the police broadcast this pathetic saga to the rest of the world?'

'Wherever possible, sir, we respect people's privacy. I' believe there were about a hundred people at the meeting when the uniformed officers called to see you. Did either of you tell your members anything?'

'I most certainly did not!' snorted Harry. Liar. With his bumptious broadcasting, he told the world yet, to the police, he failed to mention his previous histrionics.

'Mrs Penshurst?'

Margaret could have died remembering her terrible attempt at humour about burying bodies under the house. 'Of course not,' she said and touched up her lips with super glue.

Chapter 4
The silly sibling done it

Patricia drove her sister home and the two chatted non-stop about the fascinating, if somewhat gruesome event at the Probus meeting.

'It will have to be on the news,' said Patricia. 'Part of a human body buried in Brighton will have journalists licking their lips.'

'I'll watch Channels 10 and 2 as they don't clash,' said Jean.

'It's probably gone public already. I know members who will contact TV stations and be the first to post on social media. Have you checked your phone?'

Jean was on it. She ran round the Net. 'Nothing so far.'

'I'm surprised. I'll watch 7, tape 9 and keep an eye on Sky?'

'Sky?' asked Jean wondering about the relevance of clouds.

'Stick to free-to-air. Can you tape the ABC news channel? It's 24.'

'Okay.'

'And if you get any ideas about Harry and his buried body part, make a note. Our memories are not what they once were.'

Jean murmured her agreement. 'Do you think we'll be interviewed by TV reporters?'

'More likely the police.'

'The police!' Jean was all a flutter. They reached her house and the younger sister alighted. 'If I hear anything I'll give you a call.'

'Me too,' said Patricia. 'Bye.'

Jean fumbled for her door key when her mobile rang. Juggling was never her strength so it meant the keys were forgotten as she answered the phone.

'Hello, Jean speaking.'

'Is that Mrs Jean Gilchrist?' enquired a female voice.

'Speaking.'

'Oh Mrs Gilchrist, my name is Nixie Black.'

'Dixie?'

'No, Nixie, N for November.'

'That's unusual.'

'Yes, blame my mother. Are you the secretary of the Brighton Historical Society?'

'I am. How can I help?'

'I'm doing research for a book I'm writing and hope you can help.'

'Of course but look, I'm standing outside my front door having just come home from a Probus meeting. Can you call me back in ten minutes?'

'I can but would it be possible to visit you later this afternoon?'

'I think so. Yes, I'll be home. What time did you have in mind?'

'How does 4 o'clock sound?'

'Perfect but I have to watch the news on 7 at 4 and on 10 at 5. They're both on commercial networks so that will give us time to chat.'

There was a pause. Nixie wasn't used to people announcing they were preparing to watch specific programmes on television.

'Thank you so much,' said Nixie. 'May I have your address please?'

Jean went cold. She'd been told by her sister and others, and at a Probus meeting when the speaker discussed privacy and giving personal details to strangers, caution always came first. Cases were described where elderly people were defrauded by someone who presented as harmless, friendly, even caring but who turned out to be, well, a rotter.

'I've just remembered,' said Jean, 'this afternoon's not convenient. Can we make it tomorrow morning?'

'Of course,' said Nixie. 'Where shall we meet?'

'The Historical Society has rooms in the Old Town Hall in Wilson Street. I'll be there to open up for you at 10.30.'

'That's most kind of you, Mrs Gilchrist. I look forward to meeting you in the morning. Goodbye.'

'Oh, just a minute. What is your book about?'

'Sir Thomas Bent. No doubt you've heard of him.'

'Yes, of course. Well, till tomorrow. Goodbye.'

Jean ended the call and made a note of the woman's name and the saying, *Bent by name, bent by nature.*

By the time Harry and Margaret were driven back to their car, the Probus members were long gone. Allowed back inside their home via the front door, Harry sat in his study, fuming, while Margaret stared through her kitchen window at the police in her backyard or, as Harry had thundered, "it's my rear garden."

The forensic team had earlier finished the task of removing the part of a human arm and sent it to forensics. The surrounding area was examined for any other evidence. With nothing found, it was time to clean up, pack up and leave.

An officer in a white forensic suit walked through the garden and knocked on the back door. He removed his face covering. Archie desperately wanted to say g'day. He was restrained as Margaret opened the door.

'Good afternoon, madam.'

'Good afternoon,' replied Margaret struggling with the hound.

'Just to advise we've finished our work and the back yard is back under your control.'

Margaret wanted details. 'So is it safe? Have you left anything dangerous such as needles?'

'Nothing at all, madam. It's perfectly safe. Thank you for your patience.' He held out a hand to Archie who broke free and greeted the officer. 'My brother has an Airedale Terrier. They're wonderful dogs.'

'What about damage to the garden? My husband is fanatical about the plants being kept in pristine condition, especially his blood red roses.'

Patting Archie, the man in white assured the Brighton boss lady. 'Well this lovely dog did make his mark and we needed to move soil to check for evidence but everything remains intact. And I must compliment you on your garden and especially the roses.' He smiled, handed Archie back, said, 'Good afternoon, madam,' and departed with a lively stride.

Margaret's phone rang. It was Terry, her brother, the black sheep of the family.

'Hello Sis,' he said. 'Brilliant job, hey?'

'What are you talking about?' she asked with fear and alarm. The siblings maintained a love hate relationship both loving to hate Harry.

'The body part in the garden,' he sniggered. Margaret gasped. She couldn't speak. 'Bet it gave the old creep a start. Pity he didn't have a heart attack and die!'

Chapter 5
Tommy Bent under investigation

Nixie Black was on time and Jean greeted her in the Historical Society's rooms in the local library. With an unusual name, Nixie dressed to match her handle. Wearing a multi-coloured, full-length wrap-around skirt, boots (hidden), a wide belt, shirt, jerkin and bandana with a knot to defy any sailor, meant she didn't appear to be a con artist, whatever they look like.

'Good morning, Mrs Gilchrist,' she said offering her hand. Jean reckoned her age to be anywhere between forty-five and death.

'Welcome, do I call you Nixie?'

'Please do.'

'Is it your pen name?'

'No, no, I write under my own name.'

They sat and chatted. 'I assume you know there are already quite a few books and many articles about Mr Bent.'

'I do and I've read them all.'

'Goodness. Well forgive me for asking, but is there anything new to say about him?'

'Indeed there is. You see I have a personal interest because one of my ancestors suffered great financial hardship thanks to the swindler from Brighton.'

'I'm sorry. And I don't understand.'

'I've studied my ancestry in detail, and am keen to investigate specific business transactions promoted by the infamous Premier. I know one of my ancestors invested in one of Mr Bent's schemes. If the public reckon they know all there is to know about the scoundrel, their eyes will well and truly be opened once my book is published.'

'I see,' said Jean growing more curious. 'Do you have a publisher?'

'Not interested,' she scoffed. 'I self-publish and control everything.'

Jean wondered if Nixie had submitted her manuscript to traditional publishers, been rejected and so covered her frustration by boasting of her ability to survive without serious recognition, any recognition.

They entered another room with cupboards, filing cabinets and desks. A photocopier and microfilm projector stood ready for use.

'Does the Historical Society have any records of the train and tram extensions built under Bent's control?'

'I can show you where the relevant material is stored. Nothing may be removed but there is a photocopy machine you may use with a charge of thirty cents a page. Will that be satisfactory?'

'Indeed and thank you again.'

'I'll leave you to it,' said Jean and returned to her desk.

Her mobile phone rang and sister Patricia gabbled with excitement.

'We're on TV! Bobby just rang to tell me he saw it on the late news on Channel 7. They showed the front of the Penshurst mansion but there were no names mentioned. Goodness knows what the president will do.'

'Bobby rang you?'

Patricia took offence. 'Of course. He knows we're interested in police matters and ...'

'I don't believe you.'

Big sister took a bigger offence. 'What?'

'You rang Bobby and he told you about the TV clip.'

'That's what I said. Look the story's out and who knows where it'll lead. Harry may be guilty and if so, we'll need a new president.'

'Or the whole thing may be one big sick joke, Harry knows nothing about it, and he'll remain in the chair forever.'

'I think Bobby wants to use us as a sort of sounding board.'

'A what?'

'He needs people he can trust to give him feedback as he ponders whodunit?'

'Patricia, you're getting carried away. Bobby[2] finished his days behind a desk. He was a humble senior constable who saw out his days shuffling paper. He wasn't a homicide detective.'

'I know that. But once a copper always a …'

'Hold on, caller,' said Jean putting her hand over the phone as Nixie appeared. Patricia fumed.

'So sorry,' said Nixie, 'but I can't work the photocopier.'

To her sister, Jean said, 'I'll call you back.' She ended the call and led Nixie to the other room.

Patricia continued fuming. She had red hot news and her sister showed little if any interest. Patricia's news was big news. It made the TV bulletin. The sisters were part of a major crime. They witnessed the arrest of the president who might well be a murderer. No, wait. Easy old girl. That's not quite true, Patricia.

The prize exhibit, the piece of a human limb sent to the scientific police, was examined by a pathologist who wrote and emailed a report to the SIO, Inspector Charlotte Fairfax. She whistled as she read and especially so when the partial arm's ID was listed. The DNA gave up a name.

She called to her colleague, DS Petr Browning. 'PB, in here.' He entered her office, the sergeant with the whitest shirts in Victoria Police. 'Have a look.'

He stood beside her and read the email on her screen. Whistling was contagious. 'Why aren't all bodies or parts thereof so easy to ID?'

'Pull up everything on Darren Willims without an *a*. Last known address, police record, any funeral notice and all known associates.'

'On it,' said Browning and left. Fairfax hated the expression, 'On it,' and thought about how she could have her colleague delete it from his lexicon.

Jean returned to her phone and rang her sister. 'Sorry, I'm at the Historical Society with someone making enquiries about Tommy Bent.'

'He's been dead for a hundred years, longer. We've got a murder that happened this week!'

'If it *is* a murder and anyway, it's none of our business, Patricia. You need to concentrate on your book club, sewing and water aerobics.'

The phone went dead and, without a photo-finish camera, it was impossible to know who hit the off-button first.

Chapter 6
Siblings scheme

It was evening when Terry hit the intercom button outside the huge front gate rooted in the huge front fence, and his sister opened the fortress. He followed her to the kitchen where she poured him a coffee. There was an expensive barista style coffee machine on the granite benchtop but with Class not being his middle name, Terry enjoyed instant.

'I don't want to hear about it,' said Margaret who folded her arms and glared at him.

'God, you're impossible. You're always on my back about doing Sweet FA and when I finally do something, and which works a treat, you moan. What's the matter with you?' He went all dramatic mimicking her. 'Who will rid me of this permanent priest?' Back to arguing. 'You've been screaming that for years and now when I stitch him up like a kipper, you complain.'

'You should have warned me first.'

'Is that all?'

'And it's turbulent priest.'

'What is?'

'It's who will rid me of this *turbulent* priest?'

'Any biscuits?' He went looking and finding. He was good at finding. 'So tell me what happened.'

'I assume Henry is out drinking at his favourite football club.' She nodded. 'Well I figured he needed to be put under pressure. Get the cops involved. Get his blood pressure to soar and bring on a heart attack.'

'The first bit worked but what did you do? And how?'

'You don't need details, my girl. You can't confess to what you don't know.'

'Well the basic outline then. Where did you get the arm?' She almost vomited. 'Urgh, I feel sick just thinking about it. And is the person who donated the limb still above ground? The police are all over it. I had them in the garden. Thank God they've left. Tell me something, anything!'

Terry went for a second Tim Tam. 'It was all down to Peter, Paul, and Mary. They were whacking a dog for shortin' the snortin' and before they gave him a free bay cruise heading out from Tony's Schnoz—did you know most of the bay is only about 20 feet deep?—the brothers kindly took an axe to his corporation, gifted me the limb and hey presto, the pompous prick's got part of a stiff in his rose garden with a lot of explaining to do. Comprendi?'

Margaret made a G&T with barely any tonic. 'I only speak English. Didn't understand a word of what you just said.'

'Good. As previously stated, you don't need to know.'

'Why was a woman involved?'

'What woman?'

'Mary, you said Peter, Paul and Mary attacked a dog.' She snapped her fingers and Archie padded across the outrageously expensive kitchen flooring. She fiddled with his friendly ears.

'A dog is a weak prick who gets what's coming. This weasel skimmed coke from the Murphy brothers, Peter, Paul, and Mary, who run the cocaine scene from a panel beater's in Seaford. Mary is the third brother, real name Patrick, who fancies a bit of cross-dressing on the second Tuesday of the month except November when it's the first. He gets to wear a hat. I heard about the crime and punishment business and asked the lads for a souvenir, hence the arm. Now, what's happened to Henry?'

'Nothing. He's still above ground. He needs to die a natural death. Murder is not an option. At least nothing obvious.' She pointed at her brother. 'Do not send the cops to my home ever again.'

'Is my percentage still good?'

'We stick to the agreement. Once he's cactus by what the police and coroner state are natural causes, then you get your cut, not before. And your percentage drops for every month he's still here.'

'So what's the latest total?'

'I saw his super report last week and it'll be 2 mil pretty soon.'

Terry grinned. Actually it was nearer 4 mill but some siblings lie.

The police were making ground. Having obtained the DNA from the arm minus a hand buried in the Penshurst garden, they found a match on the police data base. The partial limb belonged to Darren Willims aka Mousey. His criminal record never made it to the Premier League.

Mousey's last known address was in Seaford and four officers headed out to try and capture about 90% of the criminal.

They encountered no resistance, met two out-of-it crackheads and no Mousey. He was already a building block for a future serve of flake and chips having been unceremoniously buried at sea. No coffin, no flag thereon and definitely no Lord's Prayer. The sharks were shortchanged as part of Mousey's right arm remained in storage.

For SIO Fairfax it was the regular move of one step forward and two steps back. She discussed the next move with her hipster colleague.

'No sign of Mousey at his last known and no news of any recent sighting. So we know where part of him is and that's about it,' said Fairfax.

'We know his associates,' added DS Browning. 'And we've had two DCs wandering the streets of Brighton looking for security cameras.'

'Keep digging,' she said and kept seeing images of a dead horse. Fairfax reckoned she didn't hold the whip hand but rather the whip sat *in* her hand. The horse lay frozen. Chances of finding the rest of Mousey were zero to minus zero. Nailing his attacker or attackers equally so. As for improving her clean-up rate, she sat on exceptionally long odds. Mousey's death was almost certainly a falling-out amongst thieves with little public, political or police pressure to be seen.

But Mousey's arm mystery lingered, stranger things have been known to happen, and his murder was not to be the only homicide.

Chapter 7
Harry the Kingmaker

Lionel Carruthers suffered from familial envy. The middle son of three brothers, Lionel forever remained insignificant. His older brother was a member of state parliament—admittedly an opposition backbencher—and his younger brother owned a chain of restaurants all of which were doing well if not very well. Lionel was a suburban accountant, retired, with a modest superannuation and a complete lack of fame or recognition.

Because they were snobs, his parents, both deceased, used to smother Lionel's siblings with praise. They constantly boasted of their successful boys' achievements. At Christmas and other family gatherings, they sang the praises of the go-getters with nary a word about unknown, less successful Lionel. He was also the only childless offspring. It ate away at his gut.

Since retiring, Lionel joined his local Probus club in Brighton and became as anonymous there as he was elsewhere. The one major benefit was his friendship with the president. Harry Penshurst used his charm to welcome Lionel, discovered his background and personality, or lack of personality, and urged him to stand for the committee.

'You're the financial wizard we need, Lionel. With your accounting background, you can put our books in order and have us blossom.'

Flattery will get you everywhere and come election time, Harry nominated Lionel and the boring bookkeeper joined the administration. It was hardly something to boast about. His brother in Spring Street and t'other in Southbank were quids ahead in cash and popularity.

After a committee meeting, Harry took Lionel aside and suggested they go for a drink. This was new for Lionel. Social activity and political manoeuvring were foreign subjects to him.

'You're doing a brilliant job, mate,' said Harry who could grease a fellow human as a mechanic could a car.

'I'm happy to help, Harry.'

One shandy and a Guinness down, the Prez made his move. 'Listen my friend, I'm working on a project and it's perfect for a man like you.'

Lionel's defences sprang to attention. This sweet talk had the *Beware Danger Ahead* sign erect and flashing. The man wants money, *my* money.

'This will benefit both of us and, having studied your life and situation, I believe you're the consummate chap to join with me in the ultimate plan to help one another.'

Without any effort, Lionel's heart beat faster. To him, this sounded like a con but a sliver of hope joined his thinking. Could this make me? Could this help me overtake my popular and successful brothers?

'What did you have in mind?' asked the former accountant.

'Recognition,' said Harry and left it there.

Lionel felt a fool. He couldn't respond to what he didn't understand and Harry, a professional conman, went to work. His body language changed adding intimacy and secrecy to his next speech.

'People like you, Lionel, are ignored, passed over.' Wow, those words rang true to the anonymous brother. 'You work like a navvy, do a brilliant job, then give your services free to an organization which does so much to boost the mental and physical health of retirees. And who cares? Who knows about what you've done and now do? No-one. And that, my friend, is wrong. That situation needs to change, *must* change.'

Lionel was feeling less anxious and even began sliding towards being excited. Was this the end of the being ignored sibling saga?

'You're truly kind, Harry. Thank you but I still don't understand.'

'Recognition, an award, I'm talking about a gong.'

Lionel struggled to speak. If such an event happened, it would be the answer to his prayers. If his deceased parents were alive, the entire Carruthers family playbook would need to be re-written. No slight editing here and there but a brand new and complete edition. Perhaps even a separate tome. Lionel Carruthers AO! Unbelievable!

'That sounds wonderful,' whispered the treasurer. 'But how?'

'Quite simple. If you're happy to have your name put forward, I'll nominate you. You give me the names of people who have known you over the years and I'll add their details to the application. They add their recommendation building the case for your successful nomination. The people who decide on the awards take a lot of time, but the sooner we start, the sooner you can be nominated and, hopefully, get your gong.'

Lionel thought he might cry. His move to join his local Probus now was a masterstroke. The president had given him a gift to change his life.

DI Fairfax needed something, anything. All CCTV from posh Brighton homes yielded nothing. When was the body part planted? It was fresh meat, so to speak, so it must have been buried in the last few days, even hours. Did Archie bark excessively? Nothing. Was this a repeat of *The Adventure of Silver Blaze* where the dog knew the intruder?

Harry was particular about his garden, the dog was forbidden to roam freely therein. The dog walker took the animal to the local park and occasionally to Brighton beach. Archie had his toilet locations and behaved in an appropriate manner. He was a ripping dog.

When a young detective senior constable, Blair Jack, knocked on Charlotte's door, things were about to change.

'I've done a search for Harry Penshurst, ma'am, and found this.'

Fairfax studied a report on a civil matter in the County Court where good old Harry was the defendant. The plaintiff was a Carter Thomas who sued the Probus president for an alleged broken agreement on a building development project which involved a serious amount of dough.'

'Have you read it? asked the DI. Blair nodded. 'Precis please.'

Blair explained finishing with the fact that Harry won the case or rather, the plaintiff lost. 'Costs were awarded against the plaintiff so you'd reckon this Carter Thomas chap would be angry and wanting revenge.'

'Would he ever? Thanks Blair, good work.'

The DC handed the DI a piece of paper. 'His contact details, ma'am.'

Charlotte's smile was full and warm. 'You're a star, girl.'

Lionel Carruthers opened his front door and called. 'It's me.' This was habitual but today his voice was sing-song in tone. His wife, Naomi, stared at her grinning husband.

'Have you won the lottery?' she asked, pleased to see him so happy.

'Something like that,' he said. 'What's for tea?

Chapter 8

The sisters

As sisters, Patricia and Jean were an odd couple. Blood is thicker than water with these gals but chalk and cheese squeezed in there as well. Patricia maintained a strong demeanour. Living alone, if it worried her, you wouldn't know. An avid reader, cat lady and Probus devotee, Patricia loved her Probus club because it provided a chance to get out and be social.

The club went on short and long trips with Patricia one of the first to book. Her cat went to a cattery for the overnight trips, and a longtime neighbour took in her mail, not that there was much of that these days.

Jean, a widowed mother, had an only child, a son who lived reasonably close to Mum and kept in touch by phone. She never visited him. To Jean's great disappointment, Graeme had nil issue and more than likely never would provide his mother with grandchildren. He was gay and lived a quiet life with his partner, an older man who could have passed for Graeme's late father.

The sisters accepted their respective lot in life and got on with living. Jean too went on Probus trips leaving one of her neighbours to water the garden and collect the mail. Her garden was delightful.

When the incident with the police at the monthly Probus meeting happened, the sisters were keen to talk about the event. Investigate was too strong a word but these ladies were as keen as Coleman's Mustard. Their fondness for Bobby[2] led them to seek his opinion.

Patricia pushed the subject and to the sisters' delight, he invited them to his home for afternoon tea. Proper dressing was essential to both women and Patricia arrived to collect her non-driving sister.

'You're early,' said Jean, walking away requiring big sister to enter and close the door. 'Have you ever been late in your life?'

Patricia ignored the polite ribbing. 'What do you think Bobby will talk about? He must have contacts in the police. If there's any news, do you think he'll share it?'

'He's a gentleman. He'll respect his former colleagues and treat us with his usual politeness.' Hair perfectly in place, Jean appeared. 'I'm ready.'

They drove to Bobby's place. He opened the door with a smile to warm any heart. 'Welcome ladies, please come in.'

They waited in the hall. Bobby led them into the lounge through the double glass doors with plain, so-called artistic etching, and over the floral carpet. The flying ducks, which hadn't flown for two generations, remained motionless on the wall. His wife, Glenda, sat in an upmarket wheelchair facing them. She was diagnosed with motor neurone disease (MND) aged 57 with her husband retiring early to become her fulltime carer. Bobby took control.

'My dear, you remember the famous sisters from Probus, Patricia and Jean.'

They spoke as one. 'Hello Glenda.'

She responded with feeling but these days found it difficult to pronounce her words. 'Hell-o and wel-come,' she said smiling.

'Take a seat, ladies,' said Bobby and placed a tray on the coffee table with the brightest imaginable cosy covering a pot of freshly brewed tea.

'Can we help, Officer?' asked Jean.

'Thank you but no. We have a strict rule in our home which requires guests to be served by staff.' He winked at the sisters as he poured the tea. It was served using a dinner service given on Bobby and Glenda's wedding day forty something years ago. It was real tea, loose tea requiring a strainer to sit on each cup.

On a tiered cake stand was a plate of shortbreads on top and below a collection of cupcakes. The sisters blinked. Did Bobby buy these? Surely he's not a brilliant baker.

He gave his wife a beaker with a straw and once she had it under control, he offered the edible items to his guests. Much jollity ensured.

30

After the social chit chat was exhausted and refreshments consumed, Bobby stood and announced.

'My dear, I must show our guests your beautiful garden. Will you please excuse us?'

'Of course,' drawled Glenda and the husband led the sisters from the room and outside where they viewed the garden. Jean wanted a longer tour while Patricia was closing in on boredom. The trio sat.

'Forgive me for being so blunt, Senior,' said Patricia, 'but you are a saint.'

'Hear, hear,' added Jean.

'Thank you, ladies, most kind, but I'm sure you came to hear the latest on our president and his woes.'

'We did,' said Patricia, 'and do please continue.'

Bobby looked at the two almost eager siblings. 'My sources tell me they've identified the remains. It belongs to a small-time crook and no trace of the rest of him has been found.'

'He's dead,' said Patricia.

'Shhhh,' shushed Jean.

'The police are looking for the rest of the crim and who may have done him in. I'll be surprised if they find either. And my guess is that our president had nothing whatsoever to do with the death, dismemberment, or the burial. Ladies, we can sleep soundly in our beds tonight.'

He smiled, the visitors smiled and the front door bell sounded.

Bobby stood. 'Excuse me, ladies. I'll be back in a mo.'

The retired police officer left and happy sounds drifted into the garden.

'We should go,' said Jean.

'What, sneak down the side of the house like thieves scarpering after a break and enter?'

Jean wondered about her sister's TV habits. Bobby appeared. 'Come in ladies and meet our granddaughters.'

In the loungeroom, a middle-aged woman who looked a lot like Glenda, stood with two young teenage girls, twins, who were either side of their gran.

Bobby introduced them all and then, for the older sisters, the scene became awkward. Patricia saved the day.

'We must go, Senior.' She blew a kiss to Glenda.

He protested but Jean took her sister's cue.

'It's been lovely visiting you, Glenda,' said Jean who followed her sister to the hall. 'Goodbye ladies,' she called and the others called their farewells.

Bobby opened the front door. 'Sorry about that, ladies, but Glenda loves having the girls visit.'

'And so she should,' said Jean. 'You have a lovely family, sir, and your beautiful granddaughters are lucky to have such wonderful grandparents.'

Patricia joined in. 'And thank you for a smashing afternoon tea.' She spoke softly. 'Did you really bake those cakes?'

He laughed and waved as they headed to the car.

It was a short journey to Jean's home and the sisters spoke about the latest body part news, and even more about Glenda and her condition. It was a moving subject.

'I can see how going to Probus is a godsend for Bobby,' said Jean. 'Two hours a month is his escape valve. That man really is a saint. I know families where a relative like Glenda is placed in a care home and usually because some families are simply unable to cope.'

'And he has the support of his daughter and granddaughters.'

The car stopped and Jean remained seated. She unlocked her seat belt and pondered.

'Penny for them,' said Patricia.

'There are Probus members who have multiple grandkids. Bobby[2] has two and Virginia Whatshername has eleven.'

'And your point is?'

'Our parents would be disappointed in us. Thanks to us or no thanks to us, our family tree is withering on the vine.'

'At least your mixed metaphors are thriving and don't forget, you have a son.'

Jean didn't reply. When she did it hurt her to speak. 'I've never told you but Graeme waited until he was 33 before he told us he was gay.'

Patricia could have said, 'He told me when he was a teenager,' but didn't. She knew that would hurt her sister and then some.

'I've never stopped wondering if I did or didn't do something which made him prefer his own sex.'

'Oh please, Jean, stop with the genetic nonsense!' Her sharp words stung. Patricia backpedalled. 'Look, the experts can't agree on why people are who they are with their sexual orientation. They seem to agree on one thing and that is parents are not to blame.' She paused knowing the pain her sister endured. 'I repeat, you are not to blame.'

The silence lingered. 'I think God has a lot to answer for.' Jean was off on her free range thinking. She'd been pondering the subject for decades. 'If he made us and some of us are different, you know, in our sexual orientation, then that's down to him. He made us that way. So for him to make rules which criticize or even forbid gay love, then I reckon that's cruelty with a capital C.'

There was a pause. 'At least you've got a family,' said Patricia.

Jean nodded. The pair sat in silence and might still be there if Jean's neighbour hadn't come along with her weekly shop. She stopped and stared prompting Jean to open the door and hop out.

'Thanks for the lift, Patricia.'

At her unit, Patricia fed her cat, Frankie, poured a white wine and sat in her favourite chair. This was one of her reflective moments. They often made her sad. But by sticking to her motto, *Keep busy*, she found miserable times were pushed aside.

She dreaded becoming bedridden. Not being able to get about, go to Probus and keep busy were negative thoughts she couldn't escape. Being emotionally sad, she found such fears hurt more than stiff joints.

The wine didn't help. She tried alcohol before as a sedative but being dopey didn't solve anything, and the hangover compounded her grief. Not that she was drunk, perhaps maudlin.

It started to rain. She knew she had to get up and prepare a meal. She always cooked something even if only a poached egg on toast. Her mind kept repeating. "Once you stop moving, you're dead."

Then the front doorbell sounded and she got up.

The rain became heavy. Patricia opened the door to a young woman, sans umbrella, who was auditioning for the part of a drowned rat.

'You've had a wasted journey, young lady,' said Patricia. 'I have no interest in buying whatever you're selling.' She started to close the door.

'Are you Patricia Whitelaw?' asked the dripping interloper.

The question and the tone in which it was asked caused Patricia to leave the door open.

'Who are you and what do you want?'

The girl hesitated. 'I believe I'm your granddaughter.'

Chapter 9
Nixie learns to hate

She was like a dog with a bone. Nixie reckoned her great-great-grandfather was ripped off by Tommy Bent. All her research gave her plenty of ammunition but there was no smoking gun. That was about to change when she received an unexpected email.

'Hello Cousin Nixie,' it began. She read with interest. 'In my research of our great-great-grandfather, Alfred Considine, I have discovered some interesting information. My uncle told me you are writing about Tommy Bent and you may know our shared ancestor had some risky dealings with the former Premier. If you have any interest in this and other family history matters, I'll be happy to share my knowledge. Likewise, if any of your relatives wish to receive my notes, please have them contact me. Yours sincerely, Michael Blackmore.'

The offer was too good to ignore and she and Michael met in Yarra Park near Jolimont station from which her cousin appeared. The balding, bearded and bespectacled Michael was on time. With Nixie in her usual unique fashion outfit, they made an odd couple. With both being an original, they failed to think the other strange. It was a cracking day and they sat on a bench beside the footpath beside the railway.

'It's lovely to meet you, Nixie. There are few of our family keen on family history so to me, you're a breath of fresh air.'

She smiled. 'I'll be honest with you, Michael. Family history, yes but not religiously so. Thomas Bent, fanatical. My grandmother had some old family photos including one with Alfred Considine and my gran pointed out another person in the photo as the former premier and developer.

That got me hooked. What was my relative, *our* relative, doing in the same photo as Thomas Bent Esquire?'

She looked at Michael who grinned. He came alive when someone showed interest, even a flicker of interest, in his passion.

'You're in for a treat, cuz. Have I got some surprises for you?'

He opened his satchel and removed a folder. 'In here is a document detailing a proposal to extend the electric tramway from St Kilda to Brighton Beach.'

She studied it. 'I've seen this in the Brighton Historical Society.'

'Ah, but did they have this?' A second document appeared. 'This is a list of the investors in said scheme which has no official markings. This was not drawn up by any law firm. This is not a government screed. It's handwritten and the handwriting bears a remarkable similarity to that of the former Premier.' Michael pointed to a small mark. 'And there, someone, has added their initials.'

Nixie stared. Michael handed her a magnifying glass. She gasped. 'TB,' she whispered and raised the piece of paper. 'How did you get this? *Where* did you get this?'

'You haven't read the list of investors.'

She did so and saw a name she knew. 'Alfred Considine.' Michael nodded. 'And beside his name is an amount.'

'£350. That was a lot of money back then.'

'It was indeed. Tommy didn't deal in loose change. Alfred's investment today would be a seriously big amount.'

Nixie looked at the family historian. Their eyes met. His gleamed. She imagined a whole new chapter in her book. Was this a smoking gun?

Michael had been on a hunt for buried family treasure for years. Ever since his wife left him citing *Boredom* on the divorce application, Michael spent his waking hours in libraries, historical societies, government archives, abandoned buildings and on web sites. His persistence paid dividends. Now, joy oh joy, he'd found a fellow traveller and her enthusiasm would soon match his. And there's a bonus, she looked seriously different.

'So what happened to Alfred's money?' she asked.

'I'm glad you raised that. My research suggests Tommy made a fortune as did his pal, Walter Greaves. And that's where things get really interesting.'

Nixie wasn't exactly panting but her interest levels began to tumble over the spillway.

'How do you mean?'

'I've researched family trees, estates, and wills. Greaves never married and left his fortune to his sister. She married a bloke called Oswald Penshurst and boy, did that bloke fall on his feet. He married into serious money, and a fair chunk of this cash more than likely came from our relative, Alfred Considine. Now the wealthy Oswald bequeathed his fortune to his son and this continued until a certain Henry Fitzgibbon Leigh Penshurst today, received his whopping inheritance. Like Bent, Henry Penshurst is or was a property developer, is seriously wealthy and, wait for it, I've tracked him to his mansion in Brighton.'

Nixie took in a sharp breath. Her mind buzzed with ideas. Her heart raced with mixed emotions.

'This is fascinating, Michael. Have I got this correct? As a result of the fraud and corruption perpetrated by Tommy Bent and his pal, Greaves, a bloke in Brighton today is super wealthy thanks to our long-lost relative and other investors being fleeced of their hard-earned money.'

'Absolutely spot on. Congratulations, you nailed it.'

'I don't suppose you're a lawyer?'

'Sorry, I used to work in Bunnings.'

'We could sue this Penshurst bloke and get back what should have been bequeathed to us.'

Michael went quiet. 'Not sure that'd work. There's something called the Statue of Limitations. I think it might apply to fraud, even murder.'

'Murder?'

'Well, if you can prove some bloke killed another bloke a century ago, the killer would surely have carked it and how do you prosecute a corpse?'

Nixie's confusion spread. *Can I write about Tommy Bent and at the same time reveal the sordid details of my ancestor's ruin? Will my book appeal if it exposes the ancestor of a long dead crim living in fashionable Brighton today?* She determined to find this character, Henry Fitzgibbon Leigh Penshurst.

Michael reckons Penshurst is super wealthy. Will he be embarrassed to discover his ancestor was a crim? Can Penshurst be persuaded to hand over sizeable readies and so keep his family history private?

Nixie was now on a mission. Find Henry.

Chapter 10

Everyone has a secret

Patricia froze. At her front door stood a girl, late teens, being soaked in the pelting rain staring at the woman whose face turned white. Wherever the blood went, it wasn't to Patricia's head. The girl panicked inside. Was the woman having a heart attack? Did the girl's arrival and message shock the old woman into apoplexy?

Patricia stood back. 'You'd better come in.'

The girl hesitated, nervous, afraid, unsure.

The homeowner suffered from shock, not a stroke or heart attack. 'I won't bite. Come in.'

The girl crossed the threshold. Patricia ducked into the loo by the front door and returned offering a towel.

'Thank you,' said the visitor who dried herself as best she could.

All this time, the women surreptitiously kept observing one another. This was a first for both of them. If true, they were the same flesh and blood, closely related, yet total strangers. Patricia had thought about this day for decades, and dramatically so on a certain birthday. Now her dreaming and thinking became a reality.

The girl handed back the towel. 'Thank you,' she said and waited.

Patricia headed to the kitchen. 'In here,' she said and indicated the small table and chairs. 'Sit.'

The girl sat as her grandmother made a cuppa. Neither spoke. The sounds of the kettle boiling, mugs being moved and tea-making noises filled the silence.

'Milk and sugar?' asked the homeowner.

'Milk please,' said the girl who wished she'd used the towel more thoroughly.

Still neither spoke. The girl was expecting the following. What's your name? How did you find me? Is your mother alive? But no, of questions came there none.

Patricia put the mugs of tea on a tray with a plate of biscuits and placed it on the small table in the corner of the small kitchen.

'Help yourself,' she said and sat.

The biscuits remained untouched.

More silence until the visitor spoke first. 'I'm so sorry if I caused you to be startled. That's the last thing I wanted to do.'

'What's your name?'

'Victoria but everyone calls me Vicky.'

'How old are you?'

'Eighteen, nineteen next month.'

'Any siblings?'

'Two older brothers.' Ever so slightly, Patricia flinched. She couldn't bring herself to ask the tough questions. 'You have three grandchildren,' said the visitor. 'One of them has a son making you a great-grandmother.'

The great-grandmother's heartbeat kicked. From at times a lonely unmarried woman, she now had a family. Overnight. Instantly. It was time to jump in at the deep end.

'What is your mother's name?'

'Christine.'

'Is she still alive?' Patricia cringed.

The girl nodded and then dropped the zinger. 'She asked me to tell you she bears you no ill-will and would very much like to meet you.'

That was it. The trumpet sounded, the people shouted, and Patricia's wall of coldness and reservation collapsed. She covered her face with her hands, gave out a wail to frighten the neighbours, and wept a bowl of tears. Her cat, Frankie, looked for its passport.

Vicky was out of her chair in a flash, knelt beside her grandmother, and gently squeezed her arm. The teenager wept too although the rainwater in her hair contributed to her waterworks proving salt and fresh water can mix.

Patricia fumbled for a tissue. Her emotions hopped aboard a roller coaster. Joy, excitement, embarrassment, wonder, all of these and more flooded her mind and body at the news of her new life. She stood.

'We'll go in the lounge. You lead, I'll be there soon.'

Victoria went to the next room but didn't sit. She looked at family photos of Patricia as a child and then with another woman about her age. Having fixed her face and hair, Patricia appeared.

'Please sit,' she said then waited till her granddaughter chose the settee. There was an armchair but Patricia sat beside the young woman. Heartbeats were firmly and consistently in top gear.

'What would you like me to call you?' asked Vicky.

Patricia hesitated. Apart from a few new Probus members, no-one had ever asked her such a question. 'Everyone calls me Patricia.'

'But surely not your family. Would you prefer Grandmother, Grandma, Gran, or Grannie?' Patricia couldn't speak. 'Or it could be Nan or Nanna if you like. Mum's other Mum, her adoptive mother is called Nanna. But we would be happy with whatever name you choose.'

Patricia struggled. 'Can we move a little slower, please?'

The girl understood and felt bad. 'Of course. I'm sorry. My mother told me to take everything a step at a time.'

'Thank you,' said Patricia worrying about her heart.

They stopped talking. Vicky waited for her new relative to lead.

'What does your mother know about me?'

'Almost nothing. She wasn't told she was adopted till she was twelve and from that day decided to never tell anyone. My father, my brothers and I didn't know until about two months ago.'

Patricia struggled to take it all in. 'So what happened?'

'We were watching a TV show about people who were adopted as a baby and many years later were reunited with their birth mother. The show ended and Mum said, 'That's me. I was adopted as a baby.'

'That must have been a shock.'

'It was like a bomb went off in our loungeroom.'

Patricia couldn't make sense of the last few minutes. Her life was thrown upside down. She fell back against the settee. Vicky turned to help.

'I'm okay,' said Patricia. 'It's just been a bit of a shock.'

'I think it's been more than a bit.' The weak beginning of a smile peeked from the corner of Patricia's mouth. She liked this girl. That is, she liked the granddaughter she instantly loved.

Patricia sat up. 'And your mother really wants to meet me?'

'We all do. My Dad, your son-in-law, your three grandchildren, even my Mum's other Mum and Dad, the ones who adopted your daughter.'

The words, 'Your daughter,' exploded in Patricia's brain. How many times had she thought about "my daughter"? Thoughts crashed into one another in the new Grannie's head. 'But how did you find me?'

'After Mum's announcement, we paid a professional genealogist who researches family history. There are privacy laws but this woman went through hospital records and there you were giving birth to my Mum.'

'I remember the date like no other.'

'August the first.'

'At 11.24 am.'

Silence took over. 'You've remembered.'

'Like it was this morning.'

Patricia struggled to stand and walked to a glass covered cupboard. She opened a drawer and removed a small box. She fiddled with the contents, withdrew an old photo about three inches by three inches with a white border. She offered the photo to her granddaughter.

Vicky's eyes widened. 'Is that you and my Mum?'

Patricia fought back tears. 'That's the only photo I have.'

The tears began in earnest and the women hugged with feeling.

More talk, more tears and as she left, the young woman removed an envelope and placed it on the small table at the front door. 'This is a simple family tree for you.'

The rain stopped and Patricia offered her granddaughter a lift. She politely declined. Once Victoria left and Patricia found herself able to breathe in a way which could be described as normal, she took out the screed in the envelope and read.

Chapter 11
A new suspect

The police were treading water. They identified the body part but couldn't locate its owner. He was long gone. The small-time crim had been fed to the sharks and nobody grieved his disappearance. Officers worked on other cases and the Penshurst couple were left in peace.

But that up and coming Detective Senior Constable, Blair Jack, pushed her boss to interview Harry's former business partner.

'Carter Thomas has a mighty powerful motive to embarrass or harm Harry Penshurst,' said the young detective. 'He needs to be seen.'

'Okay, you win,' said the DI and the females went to interview him. His middle-class Bentleigh home featured a pristine homemade garden, front, back and sides, akin to a professional haircut. The two female officers rang the doorbell and a woman appeared from around the side. 'Can I help you?'

The police explained their mission.

'Carter's around the back. Will you follow me?'

Harry's arch-enemy was kneeling in his back garden attacking weeds in a vegetable patch. He removed his gloves to shake hands with the officers. They all sat on a patio with Mrs Thomas providing a cool drink.

'We're interviewing people who have known Harry Penshurst,' said DI Fairfax.

Carter scoffed. 'Is he dead? Please give me the good news.'

His wife reprimanded her husband. The DI jumped in.

'When was the last time you attended Harry Penshurst's property?'

'Ages ago. Is this about the body part in his garden?'

'What do you know about it?'

'Only what I saw on the news. Have you arrested the lying slug and if not, why not?'

'Where were you last Tuesday evening?'

'Is this a formal interview? If so, where's the warning and my solicitor?'

Fairfax grew impatient. Doubly so because she was doing something risky. 'This is a serious incident, Mr Thomas, and if you continue to treat it in a flippant manner, you could be charged with wasting police time.'

'Tell him, Carter,' said his wife.

The gardener let fly. 'If I'm going to kill anyone, Detective, it'll be Penshurst. No-one else, just him. So when his body turns up, shot, stabbed, or strangled, or all three, better make this place your first port of call. I hate that bastard. Not only did he defraud me of a significant amount of my hard-earned savings, he then lied, bribed, and cheated his way through court leaving me to pick up his outrageous legal tab. Trust me, Detective, on the body part buried beneath his roses, I'm deadset innocent. Of his murder, if and when it happens, it's a fair cop, guv.'

He held out his hands inviting the police to place him in handcuffs.

Fairfax stood and her DC did likewise. 'Can you think of anyone who would want to embarrass Mr Penshurst and cause him grief?'

'How much time have you got?'

'Carter,' his wife again reprimanded him, wanting her husband to stop venting his hatred of the Probus president.

'Have you heard of Sir Thomas Bent, Detective?' asked Carter.

'I have and drive past his statue coming to work.'

'He was a survivor. Sailed close to the wind, made a fortune, and got away scot free. His doppelganger today is one Henry Fitzgibbon Leigh Penshurst but some of Harry's schemes make old Tommy Bent, by comparison, look like a choirboy.' Carter grinned. 'Now I've told you that for nothing.'

The DI stared at the twisted, angry man. 'We may come back to you, Mr Thomas. A word to the wise. Lower the temperature of your war with Harry Penshurst and never even think about taking the law into your own hands.'

The detectives departed as Mrs Thomas gave her husband the rough edge of her tongue. He continued to fume. He loathed Harry Penshurst.

Lionel Carruthers was a new man. None of this middle-brother-achieved-nothing routine. Now his family and the rest of the world, well parts of Brighton, would sit back and be shocked. Thanks to his fellow Probus member and, hopefully, new best friend Harry Penshurst, Lionel was on the up.

Harry called him and arranged a meeting. Lionel couldn't wait. Did his best new chum have another grand idea to lift Lionel's profile and turn him overnight into a someone?

Harry signed him into the local RSL and bought the drinks. Just being in this venue, being seen by important people, lifted Lionel to new heights. A couple of members came over to greet Harry who introduced the regulars to his friend, Lionel Carruthers. They treated him with respect. Any friend of Harry's must be someone of importance.

Once alone, Harry produced a couple of screeds. 'Now my good man,' said the Probus head honcho, 'a couple of documents to help get you involved with your national award.'

Lionel felt giddy. 'This is extremely generous of you, Harry,' he said.

'Nonsense, you've spent a lifetime serving your community helping people do the right thing with their tax and being a member of Rotary. People like you should be recognized.'

Lionel worried. 'Harry, I've never been a member of Rotary.'

Harry feigned shock. 'You must have been, you've forgotten. A professional man like you involved with all those community projects—helping the disadvantaged, cleaning up our waterways.'

'No Harry, I didn't join Rotary.'

'But you must have been to a Rotary luncheon. Even one.'

Lionel was unsure. 'I might have gone to one.'

Harry wrote on the screed. 'There you go. Trust me, my friend, the more referrals you get and the more activities you list under your achievements, the greater your chance of getting that gong.'

Lionel smiled. His dream of being well-known took flight.

'Now I'll get your application going and will put your name down as a referral for me. You're okay with that?'

'Of course,' said Lionel. How could he not support the man who was doing him a tremendous favour?

Harry gave him a second screed. 'When the committee in Canberra ask you to back my application, here's a list of some of my achievements you can mention.'

Lionel's eyes widened as he looked at the laundry list of Harry's good works. Wow! His generous and selfless life would surely have him awarded a gong. Pity Australia no longer awarded knighthoods as Harry was the perfect candidate.

President Penshurst raised his glass and proposed a toast. 'Here's to the two of us finally being given the recognition we deserve. To us!'

They clicked glasses and Lionel repeated the toast. 'To us!'

When Lionel entered their bedroom later that night, Naomi, as usual, was reading in bed. 'Good book?' he asked.

She stopped reading. Something was seriously wrong. He never took an interest in her book reading. For all he knew, she could have been drooling over *Mein Kampf*.

Her bookmark was inserted. 'What's happened?' she asked.

'What do you mean? I told you I met Harry Penshurst for a drink at his club. That's it. Thank you Hawk-Eye, thank you ball boys and girls.'

He leaned in and gave her a peck on the cheek, turned his back, turned off his bedside light, and flopped his head on the pillow. She paused wanting to know his news. When he started to quietly hum, she knew it was serious. Her characterless spouse was acting strange.

Chapter 12
The news was spectacular

Patricia went to bed shaking. Her mind and now her body continued to writhe in turmoil. Sweaty palms, the shakes, headache, dry throat, arrhythmia, and what she was convinced was toothache.

The details in the family tree left by Vicky were both wonderful and unbelievable. She knew she was a mother, had known for almost sixty years. But now she was a grandmother and, staggeringly, a great grandmother. She studied the document for the umpteenth time.

Family Tree

Patricia Whitelaw
(Grandmother)

Christine Bellamy *née* Porter   Peter Bellamy
(Daughter, mother, grandmother)

David Bellamy   Brendan Bellamy   Victoria Bellamy
(Grandchildren)

David is married to Alisha and they have a son, Jack

From nothing and no-one came everything and everyone. Just to re-unite with her daughter would be wonderful beyond words. But then there is her son-in-law and their children, her grandchildren, and then another generation, a baby boy, her great-grandson.

Sleep? What was that?

Telling someone, telling the world was a subject driving her crazy. Of course she wanted to shout her news from the rooftops but a hint of shame gnawed away at her brain. In some circles it is known as Catholic guilt.

When Patricia fell pregnant, an illegitimate child was something to be hidden. Why? All levels of society produced them. Royal families were experts in the field. Today, for little bastards, you have public baby showers and make social media posts which attract hundreds of likes.

Of course she would tell her closest relative, her sister, Jean. Could she keep a secret? No, but why should she? Jean would definitely not tell anyone in Lithuania or the Maldives but elsewhere, everyone was fair game. It would be all round their Probus club before elevenses.

Next morning she took the plunge and called her sister who picked up bright-eyed and bushy-tailed.

'Good morning, Patricia. Did you sleep well? I slept like a fallen log resting in a vast forest for more than a century and covered in an acre of moss.' Patricia said nothing. 'You there?' Still nothing and Jean panicked. *She's had a stroke.* 'Patricia!'

Finally big sis spoke. 'I've got some news.'

'Thank God, I thought you were on the floor. What news?'

'I'd rather tell you in person.'

'Okay. Has someone died?'

'No.'

'So it's not bad news.'

'No. It's very good news.'

'Well I'll put the kettle on. See you soon.'

Patricia took her time, old doubts being replaced by new doubts. Jean opened the front door searching her sister's face for clues. They sat in the kitchen and drank tea.

'Well if it's not bad news, what's the hold up?' She froze. 'It's Harry Penshurst. He's confessed and we definitely will need a new president.'

'No, no confession.'

46

'He's dead and been buried in his rose garden.'

Patricia snapped. 'Will you stop talking about Harry Penshurst. Just listen.'

Jean got the message. Patricia remembered the joke—was it a joke?—about telling someone a loved one had died. You lead into the news talking about how Fred climbed up on the roof when he'd been told not to. It had been raining recently and when Fred slipped, he fell from the roof and landed on the paving stones. Then, and only then do you break the news. Fred is dead. Patricia used the same technique.

'You remember yesterday when we sat in the car and talked about our parents never having any grandchildren.'

'Except Graeme who does not want children.'

'Yes, except Graeme, and now my news.' Excellent pregnant pause by Patricia. 'Well in actual fact, our parents have a great-great-grandson.'

Big sister left it there. Jean froze. She could see her sister wasn't playing some awful, cruel joke. But as her son had nil issue, it must be Patricia's offspring. Then she remembered.

'Is this the baby you had when I was only 12?'

Patricia nodded and a solitary tear slid down her cheek.

'What's happened?' whispered Jean and Patricia told her everything then produced the homemade family-tree document. It took some time for Jean to return to planet Earth.

'So sister dear,' said the new grannie, 'you are now an auntie, a great aunt and a great-great aunt.'

'This is wonderful, Patricia, and I agree, it's far more important than Harry Penshurst being murdered.'

'Is Harry dead?' asked Patricia with a massive serve of fake shock.

The siblings laughed as they'd never laughed before.

Chapter 13

Violence in the garden

Carter Thomas switched to planting. The weeds were eradicated and new plants would soon appear. He worked systematically. Gardening was his outlet, his way of maintaining sanity having lost a massive wedge of cash, twice, thanks to Harry Penshurst.

'Don't move,' said a voice and Carter froze. A robbery in a vegetable patch? Surely not but the voice didn't have a skerrick of humour therein. The intruder stood a few yards from the gardener holding a hand gun which looked real. You wouldn't take a chance on it being a fake.

'Carter,' called his wife from the back door. She couldn't see either man as the washing on the clothesline and various plants blocked her view. 'Cuppa tea.'

The shooter raised his weapon and whispered. 'Tell her you're coming.'

'Carter,' called his wife again.

'I'm coming,' he called back. She went inside.

You probably don't remember me,' said the man.

'I do.'

'You told me to invest my money in a development scheme run by Harry Penshurst. I did and lost the lot.'

'Join the club.'

'Now I want revenge.'

'So how will killing me improve your bank balance?'

'It won't but I'll get enormous satisfaction in hurting the bastard who led me to the bigger bastard. Oh and he's next on my list. Turn around.'

Carter found his trousers becoming wet. The would-be assassin walked forward treading on newly planted lettuce and onion seeds. They suffered and now the chap who planted them was about to do likewise.

'Look, I can pay you and help you get revenge at the same time,' said Carter in a desperate bid to save his life.

The shooter wrapped his gun in a towel to reduce the sound. He raised the weapon aiming it at the kneeling gardener's skull.

'Carter,' said his wife and appeared from behind the washing on the line and so saved her husband's life.

The towel with hidden gun was placed back fence side of the wife. Carter struggled to breathe let alone speak.

'Who's this?' she asked.

'Ah, this is the man from the nursery. He's helping me plant the vegetable seeds.' The shooter nodded. 'He's finished helping me.'

'Does he want afternoon tea?'

'No,' said the would-be assassin.

'Well don't be long,' said the housewife.' She left and called. 'Your tea's getting cold.'

The two men looked at one another. The gunman had been seen. He wanted satisfaction but now the chances of him being identified were high. Should he shoot the wife as well? No, that would be messy. He wanted details.

'What money and what revenge?' he demanded.

Carter started to breathe again. 'You know Harry Penshurst defrauded me too and when I took him to court I lost and then had to pay his costs. I'm struggling but I can help you get some of your money back, and set up the bastard to cop one serious dose of revenge.'

'How?'

'Not here, not now. Tonight. 10. The park near the Patterson train station. The trees near the middle of the park. And lose that bloody thing.'

The gunman stared at Carter with a look of warning, turned and left. When Carter went inside, Mrs Thomas asked questions for which he spoke lies. And his tea was lukewarm.

Nixie studied her notes taken from the documents provided by Cousin Michael. She was convinced their ancestor lost a small fortune thanks to Thomas Bent and his partner in crime, Walter Greaves. The wealthy developers, certainly Walter, bequeathed their immense and ill-gotten gains to their offspring which continued down the generations.

One such offspring was alive today. She discovered him thanks to her cousin. Name and address were noted in her diary. Her plan was simple. Knock on this codger's door, be polite but firm and tell him she's writing about Thomas Bent.

Reveal the details of Bent's corrupt and fraudulent schemes conspiring with Walter Greaves. Show how Greaves bequeathed his ill-gotten gains to his sister who married a chap called Oswald Penshurst. Ring any bells, Harry?

Show how this king's ransom found its way into a certain Brighton resident's pocket. That's you, Buster. And all those juicy details are to appear in my new tome. How do you like them apples?

Hopefully, this threat will induce the modern-day millionaire to pay up to ensure Nixie shuts up. In her mind, she reckoned she was on a sure fire winner.

She approached the Penshurst mansion. It was late afternoon when, in stereotypical Brighton, the wealthy would be enjoying a pre-dinner apéritif. Here's hoping.

Problem number one was access. The front of the property enjoyed a high front wall and the impressive front gate was locked, seriously so. Only a code would give access. Nixie looked in vain for a speaker. How else could anyone request admission or serve a summons? She found nothing but noticed a lane to one side of the property and set off. This was where the vehicle, make that vehicles, of the homeowner could gain access. She walked down the long lane and came to another gate. Again a code was required to activate entry. Damn.

She moved closer and stared at the device then fell back in fright. An alarm sounded with enough volume to set off the neighbourhood dogs. Their feline cousins ran for shelter.

She looked. Is there an off switch?

This was not Nixie's plan. She headed back along the lane thinking today's expedition would need a change of tactics. Back on the road, a police car raced towards her and stopped as if by magic. Two uniformed officers hopped out and approached with intent.

This was definitely not her goal as Nixie found herself in the back of the police car heading to the local cop shop. That human body part, previously buried under the blood red roses, had police on high alert.

Carter Thomas sweated although the night was cool with the temperature dropping. He arrived early and waited in the shadows in Halley Park, Bentleigh. Would the gunman, who crushed his spring vegetable seeds, bother to turn up? Would he be armed?

Did either man know the suburb in which they planned to meet was created thanks to the dark villain of this tale. Bent as in Bentleigh was Bent as in Tommy.

Carter saw the gunman as clouds moved allowing moonlight to reveal the would-be killer. Carter remembered his name, Joseph something. Spiteri, that's it, Joseph Spiteri.

The gunman stopped, looking around. Carter whispered. 'Here.'

The conspirators met in the darkness beneath some massive trees.

'No guns,' said Carter.

Spiteri opened his jacket then launched his plan. 'If you've got nothing, I'll settle for revenge and you just happen to be in the vicinity.'

'Settle down. Anger equals failure. I know Penshurst is filthy rich. He defrauded us both, me twice. We both want part of his fortune but I don't want to finish my days in a jail cell.'

'So what's the plan?' asked the gunman with a pistol stuck in his jeans in the middle of his back.

'Don't know the details but a kidnap and threat to kneecap him should encourage the mongrel to make a couple of bank transfers. Once the funds are transferred, it's your call what happens next.'

'Coward,' sneered Spiteri. 'So when and where?'

'I know his regular drinking haunts. We wait in the darkest carpark, when he returns to his car half cut, we grab and gag him, drive to some quiet place, and force him to cough up. He's weak, will try and haggle over the price but in the end he values his self-importance and breathing more than money. I heard he's begging people to recommend him for some award. Trust me, he'll pay.'

'Here's a better idea,' said the gunman. 'Let's kidnap his wife.'

Carter laughed. 'They hate one another. He'll pay us to knock her off.'

'Okay, so when does this happen? How do we communicate? I've got a burner phone.'

Carter snapped. 'No phones. No emails. Crims get nailed because of their phone and digital footprint. Never leave any sort of trail. We must never be seen together. We only contact one another by dead letter drop.'

Spiteri needed an explanation. The "post box" location was chosen.

'When I've set the details, I'll put a small white stone on the pillar of my gate post by the side fence. That means the details are in the dead letter drop. Once you read the note, destroy it. We leave no evidence.' He looked at the gunman. 'I think you know where I live.'

'Con me and you're dead.'

'You drive past my joint just before 4. If there's a white pebble, go to the dead letter drop.'

Spiteri nodded and Carter started to move. The gunman grabbed and stopped him, pulled the Glock from his belt, and placed the barrel on Carter's left cheek.

'No tricks,' he said, 'and this is your one and only chance.' He paused then stepped away and vanished in the shadows.

Chapter 14

After all these years

Patricia still buzzed two days after meeting her granddaughter. Interrupted sleep, weird dreams and making simple mistakes happened without trying. She put the condiments in the fridge and spent an age trying to find them.

Having told her sister was only the start. Now it was time for the grand reunion. 'You have to come with me, Jean.'

'Nonsense, mother and daughter is the closest human relationship. You two spend time together and I'll be part of the whole family reunion whenever that happens.'

Patricia wanted to argue but knew her sister was right.

'We're going to meet for coffee in Bay Street. Vicky arranged it all. 10am on Sunday. I don't know what to wear, what to say or what to do. Should I lead the conversation?'

'Stop!' said Jean. 'Just be yourself. You'll spend half the time crying and apologizing. As your granddaughter said, her mother bears no ill-will. She wants to meet you as much as you her, probably more. Relax.'

That was impossible for Patricia. It was as if a tall, strong man had scooped her up, gripped her ankles, and dangled her above the floor. Her regrets, fears, hopes and wishes scattered beneath her. Life for Patricia Whitelaw would never be the same again.

The day of the reunion arrived and Patricia parked near the venue more than half an hour early. She sat there doing nothing. Her stomach gurgled and scared the hell out of the many butterflies playing chasey therein. She forced herself out of her car and headed to the venue. Twenty metres from the entrance she saw a woman coming towards her. Both froze. They were sure they knew each other and Christine set off with increasing speed. Patricia got the memo. They were on a collision course. Neither spoke and couldn't because of their tears. Their embrace was strong and long. People minding their own business stared. Then it became the child leading the parent.

'Come and sit over here.' They sat on a bench and held hands. 'I've wanted to find you for years,' said Christine.

'I've always wanted to know if you were all right. I've brought the photo I showed to Vicky.' Patricia produced it. Christine shook her head in wonderment. She was a baby only hours old.

'It's wonderful.'

'I never wanted to give you up. I was only sixteen. My parents pressured me to have you adopted. I only had you for a few days.' Tears streamed down Patricia's cheeks.

'I know, I know. But it's all behind us now. Today's the beginning of our life together.'

Patricia reckoned she knew what paradise was like even if she didn't believe in life after death.

'And you've had a good life? You were a happy child?'

'I was the luckiest child. The couple who adopted me gave me the most wonderful upbringing.'

'And they don't mind you getting in touch?'

'Mind? They were delighted and want to meet you as soon as possible. As does my husband and our two sons.'

Patricia couldn't stop shaking her head. 'This is too much. In my wildest imagination, this situation would never ever happen.'

Christine took control. 'Now I need to know about *your* situation. How is your health? And do you have a family?'

Patricia looked at her daughter. 'After today I have never felt better and you are my family.' They hugged. 'I do have a sister who's a widow and she has a son.'

'And is he married?

Patricia didn't hesitate. She wanted honesty. 'Yes .. to a man.'

Christine smiled. 'All the more for our family.'

'I suppose you want to know about your father.'

'There's no rush. We've got ages to catch up and get to know one another properly.'

'He died.' Christine said nothing. 'I'm sorry I don't even have a photo. He wanted nothing to do with me after I became pregnant. He was killed riding a motorbike, aged nineteen.'

'I'm going to have to reprimand you ... May I call you Mum?'

Patricia worried, afraid of what was coming.

'No more apologies,' said her daughter. 'You have nothing to be sorry for. Okay? Mum?' Patricia nodded, her heart bursting with love.

'Thank you, my darling,' whispered the new mother.

Christine produced a recent photo. 'Here is a photo of my family, your family. Keep it, it's yours and there are many more where that came from.'

Patricia looked at the print of her daughter with her husband and their three children.

'My husband is Paul and your grandsons are Michael, he's a doctor and has offered to give you any medical advice, free of charge of course.' Patricia's emotions exploded. 'Do you have a favourite football team?'

'My father barracked for Carlton.'

'Well you might have to change because your second grandson, Brendan, plays for Richmond.'

'He looks like his mother.'

'Perhaps but your granddaughter is the spitting image of you. Vicky saw photos of you as a young woman and told us she thought she was looking at herself.'

Patricia smiled. 'I've never been so happy.'

'Right then. Would you like to come to our house for the first meeting? We're in Mount Waverley.'

Patricia nodded. 'I can bring my sister. Jean doesn't drive.'

'How about this Saturday at 3?'

Patricia nodded. 'Even if I had an appointment at Buckingham Palace, I would cancel it immediately.'

They both smiled and spent the next twenty or so minutes chatting as if they were a long lost mother and daughter. Funny that. They loved their time together. They exchanged phone numbers, email addresses, residence addresses, and more confessions of love.

Christine walked her mother to Patricia's car, they embraced with greater warmth than before, and Patricia drove home shedding non-stop the sweetest of tears. Roll on next Saturday.

Chapter 15
Harry's hurdle

The Probus president looked at his phone, didn't recognize the number and went to hit delete or block. But then his curiosity got the better of him. Was it Canberra asking for more details about his soon-to-be announced AO award?

'Harry Penshurst speaking.'

'Oh Mr Penshurst, it's Constable Bruce here from Brighton Police. We met the other day at your Probus club.'

'I know who you are.'

Margaret looked up. This sounded interesting.

'I thought you'd like to know what happened after your alarm sounded earlier.'

'Was it the moron who planted the body part in my rear garden?'

Margaret became super interested.

'I'm afraid not, sir. It was a woman, Nixie Black.'

'Who?'

'Nixie Black. She claims she's an author writing a book about Sir Thomas Bent and is keen to interview you, sir.'

'Me? Whatever for?'

'I'm not sure, sir. Apparently she's done some family research and believes one of your ancestors was a business associate of Sir Thomas.'

Harry stiffened. Tommy Bent was indeed a rogue and the president's great-great-grandfather, Wally Greaves, the benefactor of modern-day Henry, was a known scallywag. Harry admired both and especially Sir Thomas. The man had a serious gong. Why can't Aussies still be knighted?

'So what does she want?'

'An interview I believe. She set off the alarm trying to find entrance to your property. Anyway, I just wanted to keep you up to date with any development and assure you we are still looking for the miscreant who invaded your rear garden.'

'Right,' said Harry not being sure of the word *miscreant*.

'If you ever hear from Ms Black, you'll know what she's on about. Good night, sir.'

'Goodnight, said the president who now faced his wife.

'Who was that?'

'The police.'

'And?'

'Some woman wants to interview me.'

'The press?'

'No, an author who's writing a book about Tommy Bent.'

'So?'

He turned on her. 'Can you try using sentences with words of at least three syllables?' and stormed out to his study.

'I'm dishing up in two minutes,' she yelled.

He ignored her and looked up the file on his family tree. There was the wonderful Wally. Harry's mind went into overdrive. If this woman knew about his long ago benefactor who did very well out of fraud, and such information appeared in her book, would that detail derail his bid for an AO? Tricky. What to do if Nixie Black contacted him?

'Harry!' yelled Margaret. 'Dinner.'

Ordinary people say *Tea* but the Penshurst couple weren't ordinary.

Nixie's letter arrived. Super polite, almost obsequious, and Harry had to reply. He thought to use snail mail but needed to know what she knew and now. Phone call or email? Whichever he used, she would have his details. He opted for email and her reply was almost AI like and prompt.

She noted the result in her diary. Meeting tomorrow, Penshurst mansion, 1500 hours. The comms button is under the code device.

He fretted. Getting that gong was more than important. He joined the many who misquote the former Liverpool football manager. "Football is not a matter of life and death. It's far more important." Harry desperately wanted recognition.

Chapter 16
Hello Grannie

The family meet and greet was today. Patricia collected Jean and they drove to Mount Waverley. After the mother/daughter reunion, the younger sister asked 493 questions and studied the photo Christine gave to Patricia. She too was keen to meet the new family.

'So is David the footballer and Brendan the doctor?' she asked.

'Other way round,' said Patricia.

'What will they call me? Great Auntie Jean is a bit of a mouthful.'

'Stick with Jean. Here's the street. We need number 47.'

'There it is,' cried the passenger and they pulled up in the street beside a nature strip cut with nail scissors.

Jean was checking her hair in the back of the sun visor when someone appeared and opened her door.

'Welcome Great Aunt Jean. I'm your great niece Vicky.' A hand was offered. 'Let me help you.'

Simultaneously, Patricia's door opened and a middle-aged chap announced. 'Good afternoon, mother-in-law. I'm Paul.'

The sisters were overcome with the warmth of the welcome. Each took an arm and walked along the drive. The front door was open and the visitors were ushered into the spacious loungeroom where a group of people stood waiting and smiling.

Patricia and Christine embraced, kissed, and felt wonderful. Christine moved to Jean. 'Hello Auntie Jean. It's lovely to meet you.'

'Hello,' said the new aunt and, like her sister, found it hard to believe she now had a huge family.

Introductions flowed until all but two folk remained. Christine took the sisters to one side. 'Mum and Auntie Jean, these are my parents, Edith and Bert.'

Patricia tried not to cry but couldn't stop the tears when Edith embraced her, thanked her for allowing them to adopt Christine and welcomed them back to their family. Hearts caught fire.

Everyone sat. David the doctor sat with his wife and their baby son, Jack, Patricia's great-grandson, and Jean's great-great-nephew. He was a lucky boy. Two extra presents at Christmas and on his birthday were now on the sisters' to-do list.

The conversation flowed with laughter liberally spreading around the room. One highlight was the group photos with the special one being a shot of Patricia nursing her smiling great-grandson, Jack.

Photos were quickly transferred electronically and once home, both sisters would spend forever reliving their visit.

It was almost too much for the new members of the family. Happiness is welcome but too much joy may become a strain. Christine noticed her birth mother looking tired and, with a fabulous afternoon tea done and dusted, quietly suggested the visitors might take their leave.

Promises and plans of future meetings were made and the farewells sincere and moving. Plenty of hands helped the sisters into their car, and everyone else stood in the drive and waved. Patricia gave a friendly toot and Jean waved. What a visit. What an event. What a change of lifestyle. What a new family.

Nixie found the button under the code device by the front gate. From the hidden speaker came the president's voice.

'Hello.'

'Mr Penshurst, it's Nixie Black.'

'Come in,' he said and the impressive front gate was released.

She admired the front garden. Who wouldn't? It was one of those you see in magazines and hardback books which sit on coffee tables in a doctor and dentist waiting room. The cost of the plants, ornaments and water features would punch a hole in any large super fund and the cost of the maintenance was anyone's guess. Pick a number.

Nixie arrived at the front door and before she could do anything it opened. 'Good afternoon. I'm Harry Penshurst,' he said extending his hand. 'Please come in.'

'What a wonderful garden you have,' said Nixie and turned as a woman appeared.

'My wife, Margaret,' said Harry and the women greeted one another. 'Come this way. What can I get you—tea, coffee, white wine?'

'Thank you but nothing for me. I may need to take notes.'

'I'll leave you to it,' said Margaret and disappeared.

Harry indicated an armchair which Nixie could have bought with a mortgage. She sat.

'So,' said a nervous Harry, 'tell me about your book.'

Both were walking on eggshells. He wanted to know what she knew and, more importantly, what she was about to make public. She wanted to have him make reparations for the monetary damage his long-dead ancestor wreaked on her long-dead ancestor or, to at least acknowledge same.

Both flattened their cards hard against their chest.

'I've been researching Mr Bent and his activities for a long time. In my research I've found we are connected.'

'Oh,' replied Harry feigning ignorance and surprise.

'Are you interested in genealogy, sir?'

'Please, call me Harry.'

Nixie paused. 'I think I'd rather call you Mr Penshurst, sir.'

The temperature in the room dropped and Harry ever so slightly flinched.

'I've never had much interest in my family tree. I'm much more a carpe diem type of chap.' Harry heard the Latin expression at some business lunch and decided to use it to impress.

'Well, allow me to explain some of my research which directly relates to you.' Nixie cut to the chase. 'Sir Thomas was renowned for shady dealings. Bent by name and ...

'Bent by nature,' added Harry. 'Yes, it's common knowledge.'

'One of his cohorts was your ancestor, Walter Greaves.'

Harry played the ignorance card, pursed his lips, and shook his head. 'Nope, sorry, never heard of him.' His lie meant his palms became a tad sticky and his dream of a gong became less visible as a mist rolled in.

Nixie handed him a screed. 'My assistant'—thank you Cousin Michael—'is a professional genealogist who drew up this family tree. Harry stared at his name.

'Is this legal?'

'I'm sorry?'

'Is this not an invasion of privacy?'

'Birth, death, and marriage certificates are public documents, Mr Penshurst. You can access them, for a fee. It's just needs perseverance.'

Blood boiling was yet to appear on the agenda but the workers in charge of stoking the boiler buried in Harry's body, rolled up their sleeves.

'So what's your point?' he said thrusting back the screed.

'My family research shows my ancestor, Alfred Considine, participated in a business deal with your ancestor, Walter Greaves.' She held out another page. 'Would you care to see my family tree, sir?'

'No,' said Harry.

'My ancestor invested heavily in a rail project set up by Tommy Bent and Wally Greaves. Unfortunately for my relative, he got his fingers well and truly burnt. As they say, he did his dough.'

'That's business. You win some, you lose some. Now I ask again, what's the point of all this ancient history?'

Nixie's heartbeat got busy. She was sitting still but not so her nerves. 'I would just like your confirmation, Mr Penshurst, that the facts I've shown you are correct. I'm desperate to have all the details in my book to be 100% accurate.'

Harry knew his back was up against the wall. Should he give tacit approval to the data, ask for time to check her so-called facts, or lose his temper and make all sorts of threats? Whichever position he took, the one burning question remained. Will this damn book and this bloody woman who dresses like a weird fashionista on drugs, put a spanner in the works of my efforts to gain a gong from Canberra? He turned into a politician and chose not to answer her question.

He surprised himself. Harry Penshurst being nice? Impossible.

'I wish you well with your book, Ms Black. May I ask who is your publisher?'

'Me. I'm self-published.'

The best fake smile this century spread across Harry's dial. 'Excellent.' He stood and called. 'Margaret, our guest is just leaving.'

Nixie got the message from Harry Unsubtle Penshurst. She was pleased with the meeting and reckoned this would not be the only time she would interact with the Brighton big-wig. He was certain of that fact and it gave him the willies.

Chapter 17
Patricia's confession

Patricia and Jean sat and discussed the massive change to their lives. People they'd never met, even heard of, now dominated their thoughts and conversation.

'There is one burning question, Jean,' said Patricia. Her sister's eyes widened.

'What are you talking about?'

'Within our shared Probus world, who have you told?'

Jean didn't hesitate. 'No-one. How could you ever believe I would speak about such an intimate subject to anyone without your permission?'

Guilt swamped Patricia. 'I apologize.'

'And I think you should be the first to announce your news.'

'Meaning?'

'Ask horrible Harry Penshurst if you can make a short speech at the next Probus meeting, and explain the great joy you've just experienced.'

'Are you serious?'

'It has all manner of benefits. You will control the news, and you will announce you had a baby out of wedlock when you were a wee slip of a girl. The truth is you didn't want to give up your child but were pressured to do so. And the grand finale, the latest part of your story is you and your daughter have been reunited and now you have this wonderful extended family.'

Patricia couldn't speak. When she did her eyes were moist. 'Thank you,' she whispered.

'So, do you agree?'

'Yes,' said Patricia, 'with one apprehension.' Jean looked confused. 'I have to deal with that bastard of a president.'

They laughed.

At the next Probus meeting, avoiding Harry, Patricia asked Joan for permission to speak. 'Of course,' said the vice-president. 'We'd love to hear your news.' Joan froze. 'It's not bad news I hope.'

'All good,' said Patricia.

The monthly meeting began with Harry doing his usual blather and bluster. There was a special reminder of their 4 day trip to Bright and surrounds in two weeks' time. The bus was fully booked and excitement began to build. Glorious autumnal colours in the region, comfortable beds, fabulous food and wine, and a chance to breathe that glorious mountain air. Harry seemed particularly keen to go.

Business of the club done, he handed over to Joan. She made a few announcements then, without fuss, invited Patricia to address the members.

Everyone paid rapt attention. Harry was miffed at not being given prior notice of this event. He reckoned it was part of the female mafia running *his* Probus club, the group of females he believed conspired against him behind his back.

It was always interesting when a member wanted to share some news. In this case Patricia looked serious. You could tell she was nervous. She began.

'Nearly sixty years ago I gave birth to a baby girl.' Great opening. Talk about gripping your audience from the off. Every eye in the room locked on Patricia. Many women felt pain. Those who had lost a child doubly so.

'She survived but I made a decision that would haunt me forever. I gave her away and she was adopted. I was sixteen, unmarried, had no money and my parents sent me away to live with an aunt in the country.'

Jean was vague on those details. She was twelve when this happened and was told a tale about Patricia being ill and needing fresh air far away. After the baby was adopted and when Patricia returned, the sisters never spoke of what happened. Patricia continued her story.

'Each year when my daughter's birthday came round, I would have a good cry, bake a cake, and sing *Happy Birthday* to Alice. I thought of her often ... every day. Where is she? What's her name? Is she well?'

63

The atmosphere in the room was electric. Members were enthralled by this true and moving tale.

'But then a few weeks ago, something remarkable happened. It was raining and someone rang my doorbell. A young woman stood there looking like a drowned rat. She asked if I was Patricia Whitelaw. I was wondering if this was some sort of scam. She then spoke the words I will never forget.' Patricia paused. 'I believe I'm your granddaughter.'

Patricia had been terrific up until then. Serious and nervous but generally keeping it together. But then the dam wall broke and she cried. Joan and another lady both moved quickly to her and the whole room erupted. People clapped, cheered and even the president found himself moved a little bit, but only a tiny little bit. Mind you he also wondered how he might manage to grab onto Patricia's coattails and paint himself as a supporter of those who suffer. He could even add such behavior to his application for an award.

Patricia was helped to her seat and Jean surprised herself by stepping forward. People saw this and silence took over. Jean spoke.

'It's been a tough time for my sister but her story has a brilliant ending. Her daughter and her family wanted to find Patricia, their mother and grandmother. They did find her and last week a wonderful reunion took place. Now Patricia has a family of her own, a daughter, son-in-law, three grandchildren and one great-grandchild.'

Loud applause filled the room and Jean retired feeling grand. People near the sisters patted their backs, squeezed their hands, and flooded them with congratulations and best wishes. It was the feel-good story of the year.

Half an hour later, after morning tea, the speaker got up to deliver her talk on *Butterflies in the Dandenong Ranges*. Members found it hard to concentrate. In recent meetings, the police had arrived looking for the president, and today, one member gave an emotional talk about re-uniting with her long-lost daughter and her family. These were memorable meetings.

Today's ended and members moved to the sisters. It was especially difficult for Patricia being swamped with well-wishers congratulating her with love and kindness. Eventually people drifted away and Jean gave her sister a hug.

'You won't have to tell anyone now,' she said. 'Half of Brighton will broadcast your life story tonight.'

As they prepared to leave, a familiar face appeared. 'Well, what can I say?' said Bobby. 'You kept that quiet, ladies. I'll have to call you two Still Waters.'

The sisters smiled. That's what they called him.

Jean seized the moment. 'What news of our president's murder victim?'

'Stalled I'm afraid. The detectives made progress in identifying the body part but alas no trace of the rest of him has been found and I doubt ever will.'

'Does this mean our beloved president is off the hook?' asked Patricia.

'I doubt he was ever on it. What is the point of him being involved in a murder? And why would he ever do anything to damage his precious blood red roses?'

The sisters sighed. 'Disappointing,' murmured Patricia.

'Yes,' added Jean. 'We were looking forward to teaming up with our top cop and forming our own detective trio.'

He laughed with character which was both unusual and beautiful.

'Well I'll be away, ladies. Everyone loved your story and Glenda will be delighted when I tell her your news. Bye.'

Chapter 18
All aboard!

Lionel Carruthers, hopeful award nominee and Probus treasurer, pushed the shopping trolley from the supermarket to his car in the carpark. His wife walked beside him, her handbag under lock and key.

Lionel stopped and waved. 'Harry!' he called.

Harry Penshurst paused, raised a hand and was about to keep going when he remembered their joint scheme to snare an award.

The president moved to the couple his grin leading the way. He was about to call Lionel Leslie and bit his lip having saved himself from such an embarrassing slip.

'Lionel, my friend,' he beamed. 'And who is this lovely lady?'

'My wife, Naomi. Darling, this is our mighty Probus leader, President Harry Penshurst.'

He took her hand and gave it the lightest of touches with his lips.

'Dear lady, why have we not had the inestimable pleasure of your company at our Probus club?'

'Ineligible I'm afraid,' said Mrs Carruthers. 'I'm still a working girl.'

Her look into Harry's eyes caused his heart to kick. He knew she knew and Lionel didn't. Harry loved secrets and the image of a working girl.

'Well, must away and lovely to meet you, Naomi. Bye, Lionel,' he called as he left.

'That, my dear, is the man who has changed my life.'

'He's made you the treasurer of a club for retirees. If that was your goal in life, Lionel, I'm glad and proud of your success. Now the frozen items are defrosting. Come on.'

Lionel decided not to tell his wife about Harry's plan to have both of them land a gong in the Australia Day honours. Harry reckoned it was wise to stay schtum. If you blab, every second person will ask how your nomination is going. When the announcement came, if it ever did, the happiness and pride would be overwhelming. For now, say nowt. Even to the wife.

The day dawned for the trip to Bright. Meet at the Probus Club at 0930 hours for a 1000 hours departure. Don't be late. Coach and time wait for no Probus member. Patricia picked up Jean in a cab. Both had a modest suitcase with wheels and a retractable handle. Excitement filled the air.

'Christine rang me early to wish us both a happy trip,' said big sister.

'That's nice,' said Jean. 'We can send her photos from Bright.'

When they reached the coach and started boarding, the comments from their fellow travellers were often about Patricia's extended family.

'How's your daughter?'

'How many grandkids have you got?'

'Have you come back down to Earth yet?'

The mood for the sisters and particularly Patricia was glorious. Leaning back in her luxurious seat, it was delightful not to have to drive and instead, to talk about her long lost daughter who now was found. Having an extended family was a fabulous cake with a whole bunch of cherries on top.

It's more than 300 kms from Brighton to Bright. The coach stopped en route for refreshments, and a loo break before pushing on to the high country town, their base camp for the next three days. The weather gods smiled and everything appeared on track for a ripping holiday.

When travelling, Harry Penshurst was surprisingly quiet. On previous trips his voice was a constant nuisance but not today. Why?

Not long after they departed Brighton, a text bobbed up on his phone. After meeting Lionel and Naomi in the car park, he attended a meeting with his solicitor. Harry explained the proposed Tommy Bent book from the woman in alternative clothing, Nixie Black.

Harry's massive concern was about any link between his shady ancestor and Nixie's ancient relative. *Did my flesh and blood do mischief to her ancestor? Will she print that information in her book? Will that damage my chances of a gong?*

Harry's solicitor sent a text with Harry's options.

1. Do nothing and hope your good name is not touched.
2. Threaten to sue if Harry is defamed in any way and
3. Offer an inducement to delete any mention of Harry's name.

That text was why the president had fallen silent on the bus. He was between a rock and a hard place. Nixie Black could turn out to be the reason he failed to win a gong. Damn, damn, and double damn.

The group arrived at base camp, a 3-star hotel in Bright. The sisters shared, found their room, and unpacked. 'How's your bed?' asked Jean seeing her sister doing some mattress testing.

'Feels fine. Yours?'

'Good. I'm starving. What time do we eat?'

'Not sure. You go. I'll tell my daughter we've arrived safe and sound.'

'Ooooh,' from Jean. 'Guess who's under the thumb now she's found her long lost family?' Patricia frowned. 'I'm only joking. It's lovely you've got someone who cares about you. I'll see you in the dining room.' At the door, Jean called. 'Please give my niece my love.'

Margaret Penshurst didn't want to go on the Probus trip. The company of some of the members, her friends, and the places they would visit were major attractions. But the down side, the real bummer of the trip was putting up with her husband. She wondered about him falling from a mountain and tragically breaking his neck. Could she arrange that and remain above suspicion? Did she have the acting skills to appear distraught when the news of his demise became known, and she was secretly delighted?

After dinner, she enjoyed a drink in the bar with a few members and retired. Unlike back in their Brighton mansion, here they shared a room. But where was Henry? She didn't know or care. She dressed for bed, retired, and fell asleep.

She woke at 10.45pm to silence. No snoring from the other bed. She had made sure their room was a twin. But where is he? Probus members are retirees with many in their seventies or older. These folk are not late night revellers. Harry enjoys a drink but even he would have hit the sack by now.

She put on a robe and slippers and went downstairs. Has he wandered off into the bush and been attacked by a mob of kangaroos? Was this going to be the perfect trip? Harry is cactus with no fault attributed to Margaret meaning she was set to inherit big bucks.

If something had happened to her husband, Margaret needed to show she at least tried to find him.

She reached reception with the *Closed* sign on display. The hotel slumbered. There was a soft light inside so she opened the door. The bell on the counter existed for such a situation as this. My husband's missing. Do we call the police, set up a search party or what?

About to shake the bell, she heard a sound behind the office door, it sounded unusual and Margaret hesitated. Was that Henry? It couldn't be. She stepped forward, knocked softly on the door then opened it. Bingo. Hubby located.

The missing president was found although not as he would want to be. *In flagrante delicto* is a Latin term meaning *in blazing offence* or colloquially, *you're nicked my son*. At times, the expression means someone is sprung doing the business. Such was the case in this case. Harry was having it away with the female proprietor of the hotel.

The lights were out in the office but when Margaret opened the door, the dim light in Reception illuminated the performers on stage. Well, on the carpet.

Harry had his back to the door but Margaret would recognize those cheeks at midnight on a desolate moor in a pea souper.

'Henry!' she hissed with a rising inflection and his posterior wanted to scream.

'That's it,' she said. 'You're cooked, mate. This is going to cost you the house, your super and probably both. Hold still please.'

The flash from her phone was not so much for any divorce proceedings, more for humiliation and revenge. She hit the photo button twice.

She slammed the door, went upstairs, and after locking the door to ~~their~~ her room, went back to bed. Where Harry kipped that night was down to him.

69

If he reckoned he was in hot water now, he was not to know that earlier that day, Carter Thomas placed a small white stone on the gate post next to his side fence. Gunman Joseph Spiteri drove past the property just before 4pm every afternoon to see if there was a message. Today there was. He needed to go to the agreed dead-letter drop and discover the instructions for the kidnap, torture, robbery, and possible extermination of the pants-down president.

Harry was in more trouble than Burke and Wills.

He was reluctant to turn up for breakfast. Dressed in the clothes he wore yesterday, unshaven when his lifelong habit was to show his face to the world with nary a whisker in view, this trip was a major blot on his copybook. And all because he tried to prove he was still a man. Even that scored a D-. His paramour took pity and gave him the storeroom under the stairs.

In the morning he begged for a master key and managed to access his room, where he had a shower, shave, and shoe shine. Heading downstairs, he bumped into Lionel Carruthers, his co-conspirator in conning the Canberra-based officials doling out awards. If there was one for being a pompous prick, Harry was a shoe-in.

'Harry, good morning,' beamed Lionel delighted to bump into his new best friend. 'We didn't see you at breakfast.'

'Gippy tummy,' said the president and tried to slip away.

'I've been thinking about our joint application,' said Lionel.

'Shhhh,' hissed Harry as three members approached. He led Lionel to one side. 'I've told you, this must be kept top secret.'

'Sorry,' muttered the embarrassed, almost ashamed Lionel.

'You so deserve this honour but if people know I'm helping you, they'll all want my help. I've chosen you because I can trust you. Now please, zip it. Okay?'

'Of course. I'm most dreadfully sorry, Harry.'

The president patted the distressed man's arm. 'Good man,' he said and headed off for a feed.

Chapter 19
The cops get a lead

The Murphy brothers, Peter, Paul and Patrick, the latter aka Mary, were always on the police radar, often interviewed, occasionally arrested but never charged and convicted. Their drug empire was more a drug scrapyard. Brains and big-thinking were not a part of their collective DNA. Peter, the oldest and leader, wanted to get involved with the serious players but until that happened, hired muscle was more their line, and nicking motors proved a nice little side earner.

The latter turned out to be their undoing. They'd taken a newish BMW from a driveway where the homeowner had set up some expensive electronic surveillance. Coupled with a GPS tracker planted on the vehicle, meant that when the owner called the cops, he was able to give them location instructions. Mary was driving and when the lights and siren appeared in their rear mirror, evasion plan #2 swung into action.

They made a sudden left turn. Peter and Paul alighted fleeing in separate directions never to be found that night. Mary had bad luck and was nicked. He was wearing a smart little midi dress with cream blouse and the police found the interview tricky.

How could they be serious when the hardened crim looked like a fugitive from a *Carry On* film. Mary's big mistake was having a matching handbag from which the police retrieved his mobile. That was sent for analysis and data retrieved. Mary eventually got bail and went home to change.

The results of his/her phone proved interesting which led to DS Browning, he of the immaculate white shirt fame, walking into Detective Inspector Charlotte Fairfax's office with some news.

'Morning ma'am.' He saw her face and remembered. 'Boss.'

'What have you got?'

'Remember the severed arm buried in that Brighton back yard?'

'Rear garden,' she corrected him.

'Sorry, rear garden, well uniform arrested a car thief, cross-dresser as it turns out, and his phone gave up some interesting numbers.'

'And?'

'One of them is a bloke called Terence Twomey.'

'Never heard of him.'

'You've heard of his sister, Margaret Penshurst, wife of Henry, call me Harry, he of the aforementioned rear garden in Brighton.'

The DI leant back in her ergonomic chair. 'I don't believe in coincidences but I do love them.'

'You reckoned it was a cold case in the making but this admittedly very small lead, might be the straw that breaks the chopped arm's back.'

'Where did you go to school?' she asked, looking askance. 'You have a fine ability, Detective Sergeant, to butcher your mother's tongue.'

Browning grinned. 'Thank you, ma'am, *boss*.'

'Good work,' she said. 'Follow up Mr Twomey and see if he deals not only in stolen car parts but also in stolen body parts.'

Unknown to Harry Penshurst, this latest "coincidence" had the potential to ruin his plan to receive a gong. He was already deeply morose after his dim Bright adventure. Were the walls closing in on the Probus big wig? If only he knew.

Terry Twomey sailed close to the wind but avoided police with a natural skill. Always on the lookout for an easy quid, buck, he often pondered how he might acquire some of his brother-in-law's riches. His sister made it abundantly clear, if Terry could arrange her husband's demise without anything coming back on her, she would reward her sibling and reward him well.

Snaffling part of the weasel Willims' body part seemed brilliant. Popping said chopped arm in the roses for the hound to uncover, turned out a masterstroke. The cops invaded Harry's prized rose bushes, found the hacked body part and, fingers crossed, at the very least, caused the brother-in-law huge embarrassment. Sadly, that didn't lead to a heart attack, stroke, or other bodily malfunction. God only knows, it was worth a try and Terry tried.

No luck so far for Terry, and no luck today for the police when DS Petr Browning and DC Blair Jack found Terry's last known address and tapped on the door. This residence looked exactly like his sister's in Brighton apart from the fact it didn't. Not even remotely. Even the three-ply door shook when the police knocked.

Terry knew they were cops before they spoke. Their badges and voices were fired at his face.

'Terence Twomey?' asked the DS.

'Who?' the thief replied, genuinely, as the last person to call him Terence was his school headmaster (principal) nearly 50 years ago just before Tel was expelled.

'We have a few questions, sir.'

Sir? That's an upgrade.

'About what?'

'We can do it here or down at the nick. What'll it be?'

Some choice. Having cops in his tip, anywhere, was appalling but marginally better than riding in a car with a couple of pigs and sitting in one of their interview rooms. He turned and walked inside. The police looked at one another and followed.

Finding somewhere clean to sit proved impossible. They stood.

'What's your connection with Patrick Murphy?' asked the DS.

'Never heard of him.'

'How come he's got your number in his phone?'

'Oh, you mean Mary?'

That threw the police momentarily until they remembered Patrick's fondness for female threads.

'The same,' replied Browning wanting straight talking. 'What's your connection?'

Terry shrugged. 'Tenuous,' he said surprising the visitors with his vocabulary selection. He surprised himself. 'I've known her for years and we follow the Dolphins. Catch up for home games.'

'How well do you know Harry Penshurst?'

Terry frowned in fake confusion. 'What's that got to do with anything? He's married to me sister. We don't exactly mix in the same social circles, not even concentric ones.'

'When was the last time you went to their home in Brighton?'

'I'll need to check my diary but it was probably a return visit after they came here for high tea. I even managed to rustle up some cucumber sandwiches and mini quiches washed down, of course, with the finest Earl Grey.'

He was taking the piss and starting to enjoy the experience. If they had anything on him and the planted body part, they'd have clapped him in irons by now and dragged him off to Pentridge or its replacement. The police thought the same and left. Terry opened a beer and kicked the one kitchen cupboard with proper working hinges.

He wanted some of Harry's millions with a passion but far less than he wanted his collar being felt.

Chapter 20

It's a new life

Patricia and Jean loved their trip to Bright although once home, sleeping in one's own bed never stopped being the best. Patricia hadn't been home five minutes when her phone rang. She saw the number and copped a thrill.

'Hello,' she said.

'Hello Mum, it's your favourite daughter. How was your trip?'

'Wonderful. And how are you and all your family?'

'You mean all *your* family.' Patricia wanted to cry. 'We're all fine and I'm ringing to invite you to the footy on Saturday.'

'Oh, that sounds wonderful.'

'Of course Auntie Jean is invited too. Brendan's playing in the VFL and the game's at Frankston. We'll pick you up at noon. Does that suit?'

'Perfectly, thank you. What can I bring?'

'Just yourself. Oh and your favourite blanket. We'll sit in the stand where it might get a bit nippy and we don't want you and Auntie Jean getting cold. Will you give her a call?'

'I will and thank you again for thinking of us.'

'We're doing a lot of thinking about you, Mum. We all love you very much.' Patricia went silent. 'Mum? You still there?'

'Yes, yes, all good. I'm still not used to having a family and one who cares about me the way you do.'

'You deserve it. I'll give you a ring tomorrow. Bye Mum.'

'Bye,' said Patricia and sat there holding the phone for an age.

No sooner did she replace the receiver it rang. Patricia assumed it was Christine ringing back with something she'd forgotten to say.

'Hello my darling.'

There was a longish pause and then a male voice spoke. 'Oh Patricia, surely you know I'm a married man,' said Bobby the Bobby.

Patricia roared with laughter. 'Bobby, I'm so sorry. I thought you were my daughter. She's only just rung and I thought she was calling me back.'

'I told Glenda your wonderful family news and it moved her greatly. So how was Bright?'

They chatted about the trip and then Bobby cut to the chase. 'I thought you'd like to know, the police have made some progress on the Brighton body part.'

Patricia came alive. 'What's happened? Has Harry been arrested? Is he in jail?'

Bobby laughed. 'Slow down. It's nothing like that. A car thief was arrested and his phone contained the number of a man who turned out to be Margaret Penshurst's brother.'

'Goodness me! What does that mean?'

'Probably nothing and no arrests have been made. Oh except for the car thief who's probably out on bail. I thought you and Jean would like to know.'

'Thank you, Bobby. That's exceedingly kind of you.'

'So how is your new family?'

'They're all well and are taking Jean and me to the football on Saturday.'

'Wow! The Probus sisters going to the footy!'

'It's only a VFL game at Frankston and my grandson is playing.'

'Frankston? What a coincidence. I heard from my mate in the force that the car thief and Margaret's brother follow the Dolphins. That's the nickname of Frankston. You might spot the two crims in the crowd.' Patricia froze. 'I'll let you go, Patricia, and I'll see you and Jean at Probus. Bye.'

Patricia couldn't wait to ring her sister. The news was spectacular.

'Hello,' said Jean and that was all she could say as Patricia let fly. The football visit, the buried body part news and, wait for it, they were going to play detective on Saturday afternoon.

Joseph Spiteri saw the little white stone on Carter's front fence, drove to the dead letter drop and made sure he wasn't being watched as he retrieved the note. He read it then, as instructed, went into a public toilet, and flushed it down the pan. The details on when and where he remembered but not so well as the main detail. The hit on Harry the bastard Penshurst was tonight.

Carter did his homework. He wanted revenge, sure, but he wanted his money. Of course he deserved it because Harry screwed him twice and that double loss in court was the killer. Getting both cash and revenge drove Carter to do what he was about to do.

The two angry men met as arranged in the car park at Brighton Beach off Esplanade. Spiteri got into Carter's car, they discussed Carter's plan then left about five minutes apart. Game on.

Harry was in his favourite drinking spot not wanting to go home. Since Bright and his pathetic adulterous activity, Margaret treated him reasonably which worried him big time. Having caught him, pants down, performing number 28, the Turkey Tango, once they got home she could have screamed and threatened. Instead he got the silent treatment, which was far, far worse. Tonight he paced himself drinking in his favourite club.

Outside, in the darkness, the cards were in the killers' favour. No moon, odd showers of rain, and Harry parked towards the garden at the back of the carpark. The assassins parked in a side street and crept around the perimeter of the club. They hid in the garden close to Harry's motor. Closing time approached.

'No shooting,' growled Carter. 'The revenge is not his death but his loss of money. Got it?'

Spiteri fondled his Glock. 'Agreed but if he won't pay, he will pay, with this.' The firearm appeared.

Carter's anger erupted. 'There's no point in gaining our cash if we end up in jail. Now put it away and keep down.'

Harry cracked a break when someone came out of the back door of the club and the killers discovered the sensor lights in the car park. If a thief crept around trying doors, bang, any movement lit up the area with powerful floodlights.

Carter swore.

'Nice one,' said Spiteri. 'What now?'

'We wait. If he's alone, we strike.'

The rear door of the club opened and members headed towards their cars. One guest tried his car key, reckoned he was over the limit and rang for an Uber. 'Goodnight,' rang out as cars were flooded with light.

'He's coming,' whispered Carter and crouched lower. 'Wait for my signal.'

'What signal?' asked a sarcastic and mentally unbalanced Spiteri. 'Flashing light, morse code, flags or smoke?'

Carter slapped the shoulder of his fellow would-be criminal as Harry headed straight for them. A few cars started up and drove off. One shone its powerful headlights on the vegetation in which the two angry men were crouched, hiding.

Harry reached his car and just as he took out his key and Carter raised his flag to start the grand prix attack, Harry kept walking. Carter froze.

The Probus boss stepped into the garden, whipped out his Bright special weapon, and relieved himself. The killers were gobsmacked. Their good luck saw Harry's stream pass just to their left. Carter decided to wait until the Bladder Empty sign popped up. No fun kidnapping someone in mid-flow. Friendly fire or something like that must be avoided.

The peeing paused and Carter went to signal just as a voice rang out. 'Harry!'

Mr Penshurst, hopefully soon to have AO after his name, turned.

'Gordon,' he replied. 'What's up?'

'I'm pissed, mate. Any chance of a lift?'

'Sure, get in.' As he opened the doors, the would-be attackers knew it was abort mission time. Harry's words carried in the night air. 'Tell me, Gordon, have you ever thought about being nominated for a gong?

Chapter 21
Two amateur sleuths

The sisters wanted to contribute to the afternoon tea at the football and argued about their share. Christine needed persuading because she had the thermos and sandwiches covered.

'What about sweets?' asked Patricia. 'Jean's a whiz at cupcakes.'

'Okay,' laughed Christine, 'but we're going to the footy, Mum, not having a picnic.'

'I found my father's old Carlton beanie. Should I bring that too?'

'Don't you dare. We'll have Tiger scarves for you and Auntie Jean.'

The family car was twice the size of Patricia's and with Paul and Christine up front, there was plenty of room in the back for the sisters and granddaughter/great-niece Vicky. She would have preferred going out with her friends and especially with a boy she was keen on but for the sake of her new family, the footy it was.

They settled in the grandstand and sat on their rugs. Patricia had shared Bobby's police news with her sister and brought her small binoculars to ostensibly watch her grandson when he was at a far end of the ground. The truth was that she and Jean would take it in turns to scan the crowd looking for two middle-aged gents, both with a rough and lived-in appearance. Were they involved in the buried body part mystery?

'Wow, Grandma,' said Vicky when Patricia produced her spyware. 'You're really cool.'

Patricia smiled and started her subtle investigation work. The Tigers won, grandson Brendan played a blinder, Jean's cupcakes went down a storm and only the unsighted crims put a dampener on the afternoon. They might have been there but Patricia wasn't aware one of them may have been sporting a skirt.

In fact the criminal acquaintances were not watching the Dolphins. Terry caught the train to Middle Brighton having first checked to see if the coast was clear. She became anxious when he told her about two coppers in plainclothes. The siblings refused to discuss details on the phone.

'What's happened?' she asked when he arrived, doubly worried.

He explained.

'I warned you about those Murphy brothers,' she said. 'Don't go near them ever again. We'll try something else *after* I approve it. Clear?'

He saw she was serious and nodded.

'So how is the husband of the century?' asked Terry.

'In Bright, I caught him and some hag playing doctors and nurses.'

'You're kidding.'

'More pathetic than revolting.' She showed him the photos.

'Not his best angle. Have you put them online?'

'I threatened him with that and with divorce which scared the shit out of him.'

'And?'

'I'm keeping my powder dry but God knows, I want the bugger dead.'

'Well Peter, Paul and Mary are ready, willing and able.'

'No!' she shouted. 'We need to make this look like an accident.'

Lionel Carruthers frequented his local library now he was retired. He used the public computers to explore his interest in railways. His wife found the subject beyond boring. He joined the ARHS, the Australian Railway Historical Society, but found it hard to make friends.

Most members were interested in locomotives and their capacities, their technical qualities. Crankshafts, pistons, boilers, and brakes. He was a fan of stations, abandoned lines, timetables and tickets.

He did some searches on different sites then stopped for the day. Walking home, he heard his name. A bloke he first met at Probus was sitting at an outdoor table having a coffee.

'Lionel, come and join me.'

The chap extended his hand and they shook.

'I'm so sorry,' said Lionel. 'I've forgotten your name.'

'Cliff,' said Clifford who waved to the young waitress. 'Another coffee please, Ingrid,' who looked to Lionel for his order. 'My treat,' said Cliff and Lionel overdid his thanks.

'I haven't seen you at Probus lately,' said Lionel. 'Have you been ill?'

'No, just sick of that horrible man.'

Lionel blanched. Surely not his new best friend, Mr President.

'Oh?' said Lionel waiting for more detail.

'Sure you won't have a muffin? They're exceptionally good.'

'No thank you, coffee's fine and I much appreciate your kindness.'

Cliff waved a hand as in "think nothing of it."

'So I gather you're still a Probus member.' he said.

'Yes but I'm sorry to hear you've chosen to leave.'

'I had no choice. That prick of a man drove me away. If I hadn't left I'd have been up on a charge of assault causing grievous bodily harm.'

This was more than serious and a shocked and distressed Lionel sat there dumbfounded. He wanted specifics and was about to ask when his coffee arrived and their conversation stalled.

Lionel stirred his coffee. 'You were saying?' he asked. 'About the president I mean.'

'Don't get me started. He's rude to people, puts them down, poor Joan the VP is treated like some underling, and he treats women in a sexist and demeaning manner.'

Lionel gasped, his body doing odd things. This cannot be true. Sure, he thought Harry was bullish and brash but under that bluster was a good man. Margaret, his wife, stood by him and look what he'd done, did for the lonely Lionel. *Harry put my name forward for an award.*

'I've heard he invades female members' private spaces. Why he hasn't been put in his place is beyond me. I told him what I thought of him and he didn't like it.'

'I'm sorry to hear that.'

'But the worst is yet to come. He once took me aside and told me I should be given some award like an AO.' Lionel choked on his coffee. 'You okay, Lionel?'

'Fine, fine,' said the man opposite Cliff and now in deep shock.

'He got me to nominate him, gave me a screed listing all his good works, most, no all of which were bullshit, and then swore on a stack of bibles, he would do the same for me.'

Lionel struggled to comprehend his place in the world.

'But the piece de resistance my friend,' said Cliff, 'it turns out he's played the same game with others and never once has he nominated anyone. You wanna watch out, Lionel. You could be his next victim.'

'Thanks for the tip,' muttered the treasurer, and gulped his coffee so as to leave. He got on his way as politely and as calmly as he could.

Walking home, Lionel staggered a little such was his distress at learning the news about Harry. If true, the president was not his friend but his abuser. *He abused my friendship and took advantage of me.*

'Are you all right, sir?' asked a man older than Lionel, a chap using a walking stick.

'Thank you, I'm fine.' He forced himself to walk upright. He blinked quickly as tears blurred his vision. He wasn't angry at Harry, although he now hated him and decided he would do a Cliff and leave Probus. That was a pain on top of a pain. He found the people at his Probus club to be friendly, generous, and kind. His anger was greatest against himself. How could he be so stupid, so easily deceived? He thought of people who'd been defrauded and lost a lot of their money. Embarrassment drove them to silence.

That's me, he thought. *Say nothing.*

He arrived home and wife Naomi was preparing the evening meal. 'Good walk?' she asked not looking at him.

'Yes thank you,' he said and headed for his study.

His behaviour made her stop. She thought. *Something's wrong.*

She called. 'Lionel?' Silence. She called louder. 'Are you all right?' More silence. She headed to his room.

He sat with his back to her. She moved to his side. He looked up at her. Tears streamed down his face. She dropped to her knees.

'Lionel, what's happened? Are you hurt?'

It took him an age but he told her everything. She fumed but knew getting angry would only further distress her quietly-spoken husband.

Nixie opened her letter-box and found a card. A registered letter awaited at her local post office, now a 25 minute walk away since Australia Post sold her once local PO to a pharmacy chain. She blamed emails.

Off she went wondering who would send her a registered letter. In the post office she signed a form and the letter was handed over. In the top left corner of the envelope she read the sender's details. It was a firm of solicitors. Her heart rate got busy.

Rather than go home to read the contents, she sat on the grass in a park and opened the envelope.

Full letterhead and Dear Ms Nixie Black meant this wasn't a love letter or marriage proposal. The heading was in bold and underlined text. Talk about writing that shouts at you.

Re: Thomas Bent book and Mr Henry Penshurst

Now she knew. Her move to contact Henry Penshurst—Henry? That move now seemed wrong. No, worse than wrong, a colossal mistake. She should have said nothing, gone ahead and published her book and dealt with the consequences if and when they occurred. The saying *Publish and be damned* never seemed more appropriate.

This letter, this threat or warning to not libel Penshurst, gave him the upper hand. Legal letters can be intimidating. If she published her book and he later sued, she couldn't say he didn't know what she intended to write.

I need legal advice, she thought. *And that's going to cost money. If I go ahead and publish, he could sue for what, defamation, and if he wins, that will cost me big time. Bigger big time if I have to pay his costs. What happens when you're made bankrupt? Bugger.*

Like her other unknown victim of Harry Penshurst, Lionel Carruthers, Nixie developed a sense of self-loathing. She'd spent an age researching and writing her Tommy Bent book and now, on the brink of going to print—she was actually going to release the book electronically at first—some giant wall in the form of the law reared up in front of her. She blamed herself. Oh, and she found a new level of hate for Henry Penshurst. His ancestor ripped off her ancestor and now he was doing the same to her. She remembered a saying from that wise old Chinese chap, Confucius. She had a few of his sayings on the walls of her humble home in-between the cosmic symbols and incense sticks.

Before you embark on a journey of revenge, dig two graves.

She didn't care. That bastard is gunna pay!

Chapter 22
Poor old Harry

Things were not going well for the Probus top-dog. He desperately wanted public recognition and his scheme to co-opt a dozen or more people to boost his chances of a gong was now in full swing. All was going well.

Then, out of nowhere, some absolute moron planted a human bone, if you don't mind a freshly minted limb, in his rear garden beneath his prize-winning blood red roses. He knew nothing about it. Of course he didn't. That would be the own goal of the century. And then came unwanted publicity.

Whoever said there is no such thing as bad publicity had never tried to buy, beg or steal a prestigious national award.

I mean, seriously, uniformed police invaded his kingdom, his Probus domain, and his chances for an award appeared ruined thanks to bottom-feeding monsters called journalists. There was his name and his garden on the bloody television thanks to a possible murder at his address. Next there'll be tourist buses driving up and down his street with some guide pointing out Harry's unique burial ground.

So yes, Harry was pissed. Mightily so.

But can you believe it got worse? Dealing with the police became a nightmare when along comes some whacky woman who looks like a hippy festival on legs, authoring a book about the dodgy premier who was connected to one of Harry's ancestors, and who allegedly ripped off one of this whacky woman's blood relatives more than a century ago. And bliss oh joy, she's about to tell the world all this via her book. It's self-published which guarantees it will be a pile of manure but again, Harry's name will be dragged through the internet's mud.

There's quite a lot of it about, this internet mud, don't you know.

They say worries come in threes. Get ready to be struck out, Harry.

On the Probus trip to Bright—now we know why he insisted on the club returning to the venue they used last year—Harry resumed a dalliance he enjoyed on the previous visit. This time it all ended in tears.

Sprung by his wife as the train raced towards the tunnel, she took snap shots of his bare essentials. Evidence can be a monster at times, and knowing Margaret would have secured said photos, he slept badly. What would she do?

If she knew Harry had applied for an award and she was asked to provide a reference, she'd say nothing. Oh, but here's a pic you might like. One Bright daks down photo and goodbye gong. Two pics equals death.

The big question now stood up and started waving. Could he survive? Part of a murdered body, an evil ancestor, and a scandal on tour. This definitely looks like Goodnight Hank time.

Out driving, he stopped at some lights and looked across at the car beside him. He froze. The driver was one Carter Thomas. Former business partner then mortal enemy. Their battle in court was a massive win for Harry.

Carter looked across, saw Harry looking at him and made a throat cutting gesture. When the lights changed, Harry copped a blast from honking motorists annoyed as he stalled, deliberately. Now was that fear?

He knew where Carter once lived and curiosity killed the cat causing Harry to take a detour. This bloke was the ideal candidate to hide a body part in Harry's garden. He parked a fair distance from Carter's house, pretended to read an ancient street directory, and watched. Harry became the private detective who saw nothing.

Twenty minutes of this and he prepared to leave. Then Carter appeared. He still lived at the same address. He looked in his letterbox then up and down his street not spying the spy.

Harry saw his former partner take what looked like a golf ball from his driveway, place it on the left gate post then disappear. Harry kept looking wondering what that was all about.

85

He wore sunglasses and walked towards Carter's house. Looking through the garden, he saw no-one. He moved to surreptitiously pinch what he thought was a golf ball but in fact turned out to be a white pebble. There were plenty of them in the middle of the driveway. Harry pocketed the stone and left.

He was long gone when Joseph Spiteri drove past, saw nothing on Carter's gate post and kept driving.

Oh Harry, what have you done?

That night, Carter drove to the rendezvous spot as per his instructions on the note in the dead-letter drop. Spiteri never showed. Why would he? The man they were trying to rob and possibly murder had pinched the white pebble on the gate post. This proposed meeting was to announce the fate of one Henry Penshurst. Second time lucky for the two men defrauded by Harry. Did the old dog save his own life?

Carter waited, cursed, finally gave up, and went home. The thing that really made him angry was his insistence on leaving no trail. He couldn't ring, text or email his partner in crime. That rule controlled their behaviour. Leave no evidence for police to find.

Carter, the self-appointed boss, insisted on this. He knew criminals were caught so often because they were careless, crazy, or simply thick.

Leaving DNA was a schoolboy error and so too were texts and emails. Switch off your mobile or, better still, leave the damn thing at home. Mobile towers were capable of placing you where you don't want to be.

He pulled into his drive and saw no pebble on his gate post.

Carter fumed. He assumed Spiteri took the pebble. So why not follow instructions? The dead-letter note was explicit. Spiteri had never missed a meet before. Why now?

The next day Carter placed another pebble on his gate post. It was the biggest pebble he could find. He went to the dead letter drop and discovered yesterday's note. Then he twigged. Yesterday's pebble blew off in the wind or somebody else picked it up or, horror of horrors, Spiteri has changed his mind. He wants out of their conspiracy.

Carter wrote a new note, all of six words, and left preparing himself for bad news. If Carter is going to get back his dough, he'd struggle to do it alone, he needed that extra pair of hands.

Chapter 23

Jean meets a stranger

Of the two sisters, Jean was the one sporting green fingers. Her picturesque garden was forever being cared for with love and expertise. Her neighbours often filled her with happiness by commenting on how lovely, beautiful, even how gorgeous her flowers, shrubs and trees were at various times of the year. Local birds voted it their favourite restaurant.

One neighbour, recently returned from a visit to Rippon Lea, the National Trust property in Elsternwick, raved to Jean about those gardens being particularly beautiful now, and she decided to visit.

Asking Patricia would mean she'd get a lift but Jean would also feel the pressure with her sister not really interested and wanting to leave after only getting started. Then she thought about her niece. The garden at her Mount Waverly home appeared immaculate.

She rang Christine. 'Hello Auntie Jean,' said the niece looking at caller ID.

'Hello Christine. How are you and the family?'

'We're all well and still feeling excited about the wonderful new family we've found. So what's news with you and your sister?'

'We're both well, thank you, but it's you I wanted to speak to.'

'Oh, this sounds interesting. What's happening?'

Jean explained her proposed garden visit to Rippon Lea and Christine jumped at the idea. The niece offered to collect the aunt.

'Should I invite Mum?' asked Christine.

'Oh good Lord no. She tolerates watering but that's about it. We can tell her all about the visit after or, probably better, never mention it at all.'

Jean laughed, Christine wasn't so sure.

The weather was ideal and Jean donned her sunnies and floppy hat.

This was the perfect date for both women. Jean could discuss her love of gardening with someone who shared her passion. Christine could get to know her mother's sister and maybe learn more about Patricia from the best source in town.

They arrived at the Elsternwick property and wandered around. Being keen gardeners made the visit a treat. One would comment about a certain plant saying how they could never get it to grow well. The other would suggest a move such as a shadier location or applying an organic mulch or whatever. The women loved the outing.

There were many visitors to the National Trust property and after an hour they decided on refreshments nearby. They wandered towards Christine's car but stopped when a man spoke.

'Mrs Gilchrist?'

He was middle-aged, tall, beautifully dressed and holding a booklet about the property.

Jean had no idea who he was but a thought pinged in her mind and a flash of fear whipped across her face.

'It *is* Mrs Gilchrist?' repeated the stranger. 'Mrs Jean Gilchrist.'

'Yes,' replied Jean. Christine too was intrigued.

'I'm James Friend, Graeme's partner. It's lovely to finally meet you.'

He was ready to offer a hand but decided to wait for her response. Years ago, her son told him about Graeme's parents' reaction to Graeme being gay, and to living with a man. James remembered one of Graeme's comments. His father told him straight. 'You realize you'll never have children.'

Jean indicated Christine. 'This is my niece, Christine.'

The couple greeted one another and Christine offered her hand which James shook willingly and warmly.

'Did you say niece?' he asked.

Jean was still in shock. Christine loved being able to explain her new family. 'Yes, Auntie Jean's sister, Patricia, is my Mum. And your partner Graeme is my cousin.'

James joined the queue of those in shock. 'I thought I knew all of Graeme's family. Strange he's never mentioned his cousin Christine.'

She laughed. 'That's because he's never heard of me. My family had never heard of Patricia or Jean until a few weeks ago. Finding my Mum was the best thing that ever happened to me. And Auntie Jean will back me up.'

What could Jean say? She did indeed support her niece and with genuine feeling.

'Well ladies, this is a serendipitous occasion. Please, you must allow me to buy you a coffee.'

Christine waited for her aunt to respond. Her upbringing gave her no choice. 'That would be lovely,' she said and off they went.

Once settled, James asked several non-intrusive questions about Christine and her family and things were going swimmingly until Jean couldn't hold back any more.

'I wanted to ask you, Mr Friend ...'

'James, please.'

'James, I am wondering how you knew me, my name. We've never met and there you were, recognizing me as if we were old friends.' She smiled at her pun. 'Friend.'

'Easily explained, Mrs Gilchrist.'

'Jean, please.'

Christine beamed inside. She was delighted with her aunt's change in demeanour and attitude. James explained.

'Jean, your son has more photos of you in our home than you could imagine. You as a girl, a young woman, on your wedding day with your late husband, on holiday, at Graeme's graduation, and several more. I reckoned I could recognize you anywhere and today, my theory proved to be true.'

He smiled, the ladies smiled and their tea, not coffee, went down a treat.

But the news kept coming. Jean shed any inhibitions about her son and his lifestyle. She saw a kind, real and loving person in front of her and someone she was proud to call her second son.

'So Patricia must be delighted she has grandchildren,' said James.

'And a great-grandchild,' added Christine.

'That's wonderful,' he said. 'But Jean, you too have grandchildren.'

The tea went cold and the sugar in its bowl held its breath. Jean's mouth opened and stayed open. Christine stared unable to blink.

'Now to be fair,' said James, 'they are not in a direct line as Christine's children but Graeme and I treat them as such. Let me explain. I was once married to a lovely lady and we had a girl and a boy—my children. My daughter has two children, my grandchildren, who call me Poppy 1 and Graeme Poppy 2.'

Jean thought she would stop breathing. James continued.

'Then many years ago, Graeme and I adopted a young girl from Thailand, and she is now a psych nurse and engaged to be married to an airline pilot, which is very handy when Graeme and I travel o/s. And so Jean, you too have a varied and wonderful extended family.'

Christine looked at her aunt who took out a handkerchief and dabbed her eyes.

'You may have just outscored your sister in the family tree stakes,' said her niece. 'We must do this more often.'

Other people looked at the trio laughing and toasting one another with their cups of tea.

Chapter 24
Car park spies

Jean was bursting with news. Christine dropped her home and promised to say nothing to her mother for at least an hour.

'Hello Jean, what have you been up to?' said Patricia answering her sister's phone call.

'My niece and I have just spent a lovely two hours at Rippon Lea.'

'Oh yes, and how did that go?' replied Patricia in a super casual way.

Jean's shock burst forth. 'How did you know?'

'Come now sister, you said it. The mother daughter relationship is the closest there is. She told me of your kind invitation before you even left home. Christine and I have no secrets.'

'Not quite true, sister dear.'

Silence. It was Patricia's turn to be shocked. 'Meaning?' she asked with a parental tone in her voice.

'It would appear, Patricia, you are not the only sibling with an extended family, and your darling daughter has agreed to my request about keeping Mum until after this call.'

Patricia pondered a dozen questions. She was convinced her sister was serious but about what, she didn't have a clue. 'Please explain.'

Jean did. Patricia listened with increasing disbelief.

'Now I know my grandchildren are not my flesh and blood as are yours but I am over the moon about Graeme and James and their adopted children, now all adults, and their children, and can't wait to meet them.'

'Good for you,' said Patricia, 'and I hope you'll include me in your first family get-together.'

'Of course.'

'And tell me again. Graeme's partner recognized you because your son, my nephew, has filled his home with pictures of his mother?'

'Well I don't know about filled but certainly several.'

'That must make you so proud, Jean.'

'It does.'

'And you know what this means?'

'No.'

'Family tradition. I did it and now you must relate your tale at the next Probus meeting in front of the entire membership.'

'Oh Lord,' groaned the younger sister. 'Really?'

'Really.'

And so the family tradition prevailed. At the next Probus meeting, Jean approached the president and asked for permission to make a statement to the members. Of course Harry, sticky beak Harry, wanted details.

'It's just to tell members some good news about my family as Patricia did at the last meeting.'

Harry dragged his feet. 'How long will you take?'

'Three minutes, tops. I've timed it.'

With Joan hovering in the background, Harry relented. Jean stood and spoke. She didn't hold back describing how she and her late husband found the news about their son being gay to be a challenge. She confessed what she called her sins, expressing regret about treating her son as if he had done something wrong. Then her emotions appeared. Patricia squeezed her chair hoping Jean could hold it together.

She did and when she got onto James and the couples' children, her pride and happiness took over. It was a stirring speech. When she finished, the members didn't just thank her, they celebrated with her. Huge applause which covered Bobby2's response as he stood calling, 'Bravo! Bravo!' Other members joined Bobby in standing to applaud.

The meeting proceeded and again, the speaker copped the rough end of the pineapple as paying attention proved tricky. Some members couldn't stop whispering about the sisters and their recently discovered extended families.

Two hours earlier, outside in the carpark, a woman sat in her car observing. She arrived before the Probus meeting started and watched as people arrived and moved to the building. A few were on sticks or walkers. Rabbiting and greetings were commonplace.

Then something caught the woman's eye. In the garden beside the car park, plants moved thanks to someone hidden therein. Why? The woman in the car sat fascinated. The last of the Probus members went inside.

The woman hiding in the garden emerged carrying a camera with a long lens. She'd collected extraneous bits of the garden but this detritus didn't stand out due to the photographer's clothing, most sourced from a charity shop, and even from bags dumped beside the bin for donations. The photographer walked to a car parked almost directly opposite from the vehicle where the first woman sat observing the whole thing.

The observer didn't know why but she left her vehicle, walked to the photographer's, and tapped on the driver's window.

The woman wearing part vegetation and part odd, assorted garments wound down her window.

'Don't tell me. Are you a parking officer?' she asked.

'No,' said the woman. 'I was curious about seeing you taking photos.'

'Are you police or from a solicitor's office?'

'No, none of those,' stated the inquisitive woman.

'Well if you must know, I was taking pictures of a man who is trying to ruin my life.'

'I don't suppose his name is Harry Penshurst?'

The photographer's eyes widened. 'Has he threatened you too?'

'Not me. He's upset my husband, and I would like to find a way to hit back at Harry Penshurst.'

'We need to talk,' said Nixie Black.

The women walked to a nearby coffee shop, explained their tales of woe, and bonded.

'You know we are not the only people with a grievance against Harry Penshurst,' said Naomi Carruthers.

'What? You're saying there are more than just two victims?'

'Several more. The harder I investigated, the more I found.'

'Such as?'

'I found a man through court records. Penshurst cost Carter Thomas a small fortune and this man wants revenge and is prepared to use force.'

'Whoa,' reacted Nixie. 'I'm not going to jail.'

'Me neither but there has to be a way to get even, to stop Harry Penshurst in his tracks.'

'How?'

'I'm working on a plan. You'll need your camera.'

And that was how Nixie and Naomi became co-conspirators in their war against the president of his local Probus club.

That evening, Carter Thomas arrived super early at the meeting place. This was a make or break meeting for the two men ripped off by Harry Penshurst. Carter was to demand an explanation for Spiteri's no-show the previous night.

Carter wished he had a gun. His pocketed pen knife was his only form of attack or defence but having been on the wrong end of Spiteri's firearm once before, he didn't like his chances. Besides, he was more Cowardly Lion than thug. And his desire to acquire money from Penshurst was more powerful than his fear of his potential partner.

Spiteri arrived ignorant of the missed meeting and growing more edgy every day that his money remained in Penshurst's back pocket. It was actually in one of Harry's many accounts including a couple of off-shore numbers.

Carter confronted his "mate." 'Where were you last night?'

'What's it to you?'

'As agreed, I put a stone on my fence post yesterday afternoon.'

'No you didn't. I drove past at 3.59 and saw nothing.'

'Liar,' screamed Carter in his passive aggressive voice.

Spiteri produced the photo on his phone. 'Check the date and time,' he said and Carter knew someone had pinched his pebble.

'Shit. I had the perfect plan all set for last night,' growled Carter.

'Yeah sure, no pebble and no pay day. Perhaps we need a change of leader.' Spiteri threw down a challenge. 'You're all piss and wind, mate. I can manage Penshurst on me lonesome. This is goodbye time, pal. And you can stick your dead letter drop up your dead letter arse.'

Spiteri started to move but stopped when Carter grabbed his arm. Spiteri's Glock appeared in three nanoseconds with its pointy end pressed hard against his fellow desperado's cheek.

Carter fought back with words. 'Kill me and you get no dough but plenty of porridge. Now put that away and listen to how we are gunna rob Harry Penshurst and make his life a never-ending misery.'

Their combined rage and frustration dominated but both knew this was last chance saloon time, and Spiteri holstered his firearm. The temperature dropped and Carter explained his latest scheme.

'It'll be soon, a new venue but the same M.O. We jump him, you stick your Glock up his nose, we bundle him into my car, oh, and of course we both wear gloves and balaclavas. The back seat will be covered in disposable plastic. We drive him to a spot where no-one will find us. He makes a deposit, deposits plural, into both our accounts.'

'How much?'

'As much as his banks allow.'

'Each?'

'Each.' That put Spiteri marginally at ease.

'Then what? If we off him, we need somewhere to lose the body.'

'We're not going to kill him because there are other players in this game who will take care of our friend.'

'Other players! What the hell are you talking about?'

'Listen you wannabe gangster, the less you know the less you can reveal. You'll get your money and be rid of Penshurst all in one hit. Leave it to the grownups and be ready to move when I say.'

Spiteri wanted to move now. 'So when does all this happen?'

'Just follow orders. Keep looking for that small white pebble and be ready to strike when I give the word.'

Spiteri grunted and each in their own car, drove away.

Chapter 25

Harry on thin ice

With so many members in their new and extended families, there was plenty for the sisters to talk about, and it was hard to know where to start.

Re-connecting with her son, Jean topped the bill. She had never stopped loving him and deeply regretted not having stood up to her husband when he reacted so badly after Graeme told his parents about his sexual orientation.

Now the mother and son were on the phone to one another almost daily. There was a new game in town. Jean and Graeme versus Patricia and Christine. Both couples wanted to know more about the other.

Bobby2, the body part mystery and anything about Probus faded as the sisters and their families got stuck into being friends for life.

Probus kept on keeping on and the next meeting began with a few members on tenterhooks. Patricia and Jean were back to being keen for any news about the president's rear garden mystery and his run-in with the police. Bobby2 only yesterday tapped his mate, a serving officer, for the latest news.

Lionel Carruthers recovered from his shock discovery of being scammed by his so-called friend, Harry Penshurst, and determined to attend the monthly meeting to politely confront Harry about the matter. Tricky because Lionel and confrontation were strange bedfellows.

Margaret feared her determination to help her husband to "accidentally" die, would fail, and give her away. To whom she wasn't sure.

Elsewhere Terry Twomey, Carter Thomas, Joseph Spiteri, Naomi Carruthers, and Nixie Black lay awake at night planning how they could do him in, destroy his reputation, collect big bucks from him, or all three.

At the Probus meeting, after official business, the agenda was suspended being given over to photos from the trip to Bright. The tech expert of the group, Neil, had prepared a Power Point presentation and many gasps, comments and much laughter ensued. At the slide show, the president appeared restrained and his wife looked uncomfortable.

The speaker this month was a retired entertainer best known for his role in a well-known TV soap. As a teenager, he got his first break at the now closed and much missed Tivoli theatre, and his memories of life in showbusiness were sharp, fascinating, and funny.

Lionel tried to catch Harry's eye and ask a direct but delicate question. Harry ignored him. He had other fish to fry.

The sisters sat with Bobby[2] and he asked about their new families. When the women turned the topic to the police, the former cop had no news. He promised to report on any developments.

The meeting ended and members went home or to lunch.

The atmosphere in the Penshurst mansion remained frosty. The elephant in every room was Harry making a fool of himself at Bright. Margaret threatened divorce proceedings but she knew that could take an age, a lot of her money, and if he refused to move, the house might have to be sold, and she didn't want to leave the home she decorated with love and money.

Her brother was under strict instructions to do nothing without her express permission. Harry's death by natural causes is what she craved.

Elsewhere, Carter Thomas continued to smoulder. To him, Penshurst was the devil incarnate and only his suffering, financial ruin and horrible demise would satisfy. Carter didn't want prison so Penshurst's fate must leave Carter free to enjoy his newly-acquired wealth. Joseph Spiteri was Carter's doppelganger only more inclined to shoot first and rob later.

Nixie Black discovered frustration. All that work and yet her tome, in print form only as a single copy from Officeworks, gathered dust in a bottom drawer. If Henry Penshurst were to expire, the threat of legal action, if it had any merit, would disappear. Die, Harry, die.

Last but by no means least, Lionel Carruthers suffered a new form of depression. He'd been lied to, deceived and that hurt. He would never be able to upstage his successful brothers now his dream of a gong was dead.

To remain at his Probus club would be torture. To walk away would mean his treasurer role would be gone and the friends he made would be lost. Life could be so much better if the president disappeared. Could Lionel be a killer? Surely not but then desperate situations call for desperate measures; anything's possible. His wife said nothing about her new acquaintances, Nixie Black and Carter Thomas.

Margaret woke and opened the curtains in her stunning boudoir. She and Harry had slept in separate rooms for years. After making use of her much renovated ensuite, downstairs she fired up her Kaffeselskabet Crown Espresso Machine 1AL, worth thousands, but couldn't find her copy of *The Age*. Fetching the paper and placing it on the granite top workbench in the kitchen was hubby's main task every morning. Where's Harry?

Archie moped around looking lost. Why wasn't he roaming the front garden? Again, Harry's responsibility. Put the dog outside. She let the hound out and called.

'Harry! Where are you?'

No reply. She was 3% anxious and 97% angry. She went upstairs and to his smaller, less ostentatious bedchamber. Without knocking, she opened the door and barked. 'Harry!' No husband and bed not slept in. This edged towards a mystery. Staying out late was a regular occurrence for the balding bully but always he would find his way home.

Margaret's anger level rose to 98%. A flicker of worry tickled her brain. He's dead, Terry and his mad musical trio mates are responsible and this will come back and bite the wife, me—hard.

There were a few things she could do although ringing around to see if anyone knew where he might be was not one of them. She imagined the gossip at Probus. "Margaret's lost Harry." No thank you. 'Harry!'

She looked in the garage and saw her car. He never went out without cologne and his Merc so where is he?

Bugger. Harry's missing.

Dog walkers often appear in TV dramas, novels, and true crime documentaries when a dead body is found. You'd think novelists could find a new method of discovery. It happened again this time in Brighton close to those brightly-coloured, seriously-expensive bathing boxes. One such person, a dog walker, was responsible for finding Harry Penshurst.

Chapter 26

Whodunit?

By 0800 hours Margaret was seriously annoyed. She rang her brother.

'G'day, Sis, what's new?'

'You tell me.'

'Hey?'

'You tell me your news but in a very vague language.'

'Look, you know I don't get out of bed before lunchtime. The crossword in the *Herald Sun* is my Mensa level on a good day. So what the hell are you talking about?'

She went to reply when the bell at her front gate sounded.

'I'll call you back.' She hit the comms button. 'Who is it?'

'It's Constable Bruce from the Brighton police, Mrs Penshurst. May we come in?'

The gate opened and the same two uniformed constables who walked into that Probus meeting weeks ago, stood at the now opened Penshurst front door. They weren't laughing.

'What's happened?' asked Margaret.

'May we come inside?' The police were polite but businesslike and entered the cathedral-like foyer.

'Please, has something happened to my husband? I can't find him.'

'I'm afraid we have bad news, Mrs Penshurst. A member of the public found a body in the undergrowth near the Brighton bathing boxes and we believe it to be your husband.'

Margaret couldn't decide how to react. She'd wanted her spouse to depart allowing her to be rid of the man she not only no longer loved but had come to despise. Did she ever love him? Plus there was the minor matter of gaining control of his super and impressive share portfolio.

'You said body. Do you mean he's dead?'

'We're afraid so. You have our condolences, Mrs Penshurst.'

The other constable murmured her agreement. Both had been trained in delivering such news. Some people reacted with hysteria. Mrs Penshurst reacted in a way that definitely didn't resemble hysteria.

'And you're certain it's Harry?'

'Sadly yes. As you know we met your husband when we called at your Probus club.'

Margaret borrowed some tears from a crocodile, wiped her eyes, and struggled to know what to say. 'Did he have a heart attack? He's on pills for his blood pressure.'

'I'm sorry, Mrs Penshurst but we can't tell you anything specific. Detectives are investigating his death and no doubt will inform you about the details of his passing.'

'What do I do?' She was genuinely confused.

'There is the formality of identifying the body. Is there someone else who could do that if you don't feel up to it?

'No, I can do that.'

'Thank you,' said Constable Bruce. 'Can you make your own way there?' She started to collapse and both constables caught her just in time. 'Perhaps we could help.'

Talk about miracles. The collapse routine collapsed. 'What, now? I'm hardly dressed for any occasion let alone a trip to the morgue. Is that where he's been taken?'

'We could call a cab for you,' offered the female constable.

Margaret was lost. Husband dead, his body to identify, and a trip to arrange with decisions to make. What will I wear? My make-up's a mess.'

The police called a cab. Margaret dressed, mainly in black, and she was driven to look at the man she had long wanted to die. Job done.

You know that expression about something spreading like wildfire. Well news of Harry's death spread even faster. The media were all over it. And once one member of the Brighton Probus club got wind of the Prez's passing, the entire world knew. If a movie were made of this small slice of life in the 'burbs,' there would be a shot of someone on the phone blabbing away. The audio track would have the human speaking like The

Chipmunks sounded in the late 1950s. Then the screen would be halved then divided into four scenes and then eight. Each scene would display the same activity. A person, the news spreader, on the phone, gesticulating and telling the person they called that Harry Penshurst has been found dead. Harry is no more and the Probus club of which he was a prominent member now needed a new president.

This is where Chinese Whispers took over. 'I heard he was found in the bushes' became, 'I heard he was dead drunk outside a bathing box,' to 'I heard he was half naked and wearing a woman's high heel shoes.'

Homicide detectives arrived at the scene having trouble examining it and the body because of the thickness of the undergrowth. How did the body get in there?

Forensic officers took photos. There were no obvious signs of foul play, no blood leaking from a gunshot wound or stab or slash marks from a knife or machete. There was no ligature around his neck or obvious bruising and no liquid or frothing around his mouth.

Did he crawl into the bushes and suffer a heart attack? If so, what on Earth for? Apart from the fact his pants were at half-mast and his eyes were wide open as in astonishment, Harry could have been a happy drunk leaving this world with a song in his heart. The only thing the police were certain about was the person was dead.

But why was he sporting a piece of rehashed cardboard on his chest, held there by twine around his neck, with the words *Tommy Bent*?

The police doctor declared the body deceased but declined to give a cause of death until after the autopsy.

The homicide detective in charge was Inspector Gareth Righteous with his 2IC, Detective Sergeant Grace Benaud, known to everyone as Richie.

Cause of death was unknown but how many suicides crawl into the undergrowth, drop their daks, and place a sign of a notorious dead politician on their chest?

This death screamed homicide.

Chapter 27
Homicide verses Hamicide

Patricia heard the news from her bedside radio. It was her alarm and it came alive at 0730 hours. She would perform her ablutions and exercises while listening to the newsreader. Midway through her stretching, as approved for seniors, she stopped as if shot.

'The body of a man was found on the Brighton beach foreshore near Dendy Street at dawn. The man's identity has not been released but police believe he is a local resident. Homicide detectives are investigating.'

Patricia rang her sister. Jean used the television for her news and it was swamped with international events.

'Some bloke has been found dead near the bathing huts,' said Patricia.

'Some bloke doesn't mean a lot,' replied her sister.

'Bobby'll know. I'll ring him.'

'If it's someone we know, call me. Even if it's not, I want to know.'

'Good morning, Patricia. I was just about to ring you,' said Bobby. 'It's terrible news, I'm afraid. Our president is dead.'

'What?' gasped the woman with the new family. Shock after shock.

'My mate reckons the constables who found him were the ones who came to our Probus meeting so identity was straightforward. The media won't be told until Margaret is informed.'

'Poor Margaret,' said Patricia. 'What happened?'

'Don't know but Homicide is on the job.'

'Oh my Lord, this will hit the club really hard. Will you let me know if any other information comes your way? Please.'

'Of course. And on a happier note, I hope your new family is well.'

'They are, thank you. And Glenda, how is today?'

'She's especially bright this morning. The twins are coming later and that always gives her a burst of energy.'

'How lovely.'

'Well, I'd better let you go. I'm sure you have a sister who'd be very keen to hear the news, as sad as it is.'

'Thanks Senior. We'll talk soon. Bye.'

Back from the body on the beach, DS Benaud knocked on her boss's door. DI Righteous liked his colleague. She made him look better. Not that he didn't deserve his rank but she had ideas and blue sky thinking was not his forte.

'This is interesting,' said Richie. 'DI Fairfax from Brighton sent me an email re our body on the beach. Harry Penshurst was on her radar recently when a human arm was buried in his back yard.'

'A human arm? Archaeological or criminal?'

'Turned out to belong to a missing minor drug dealer. Solid citizen, Mr Penshurst, denied all knowledge and there the matter died, or should that be lost momentum? So without the rest of the victim being found ...'

'Unlikely.'

'Highly unlikely meaning no charges are forthcoming but it's worth noting now that the same homeowner has himself become a possible homicide.'

'As you say, worth noting. And what do we know about our victim?'

'Wealthy retiree, no criminal record, married, no children, and involved in local events.'

'What local events?'

'He's the president of the Brighton Probus club.'

Righteous became unrighteous. 'Oh God, I had to speak at one of those. Painful doesn't begin to cover it.'

'Had to?'

'My uncle Roger belongs to one and cornered me at Christmas. "The role of the police today" was my chosen topic.'

'Sounds suitably vague.'

'Deliberately so and then I copped a barrage of why the courts don't lock up the crooks and throw away the key. One bloke followed me into the car park giving me an earful.'

Richie laughed. 'Wish I'd been there. Don't forget, sir, autopsy 1400.'

Patricia rang her sister worried about how to break the news. No need.

Jean answered after one ring. 'I've just heard. It's terrible, terrible.'

'Who told you?' almost demanded Patricia unhappy to have been gazumped as news breaker.

'It must have been a heart attack. He did have high blood pressure.'

Patricia spoke with emphasis. 'Jean, who told you?'

'Oh, ah, Joan Wainwright.'

'Well how the hell did she know?'

'I don't know,' said Jean, miffed and confused as to why her sister wanted to know who knew what and when rather than the important news, the death of their president. 'I can't believe he was murdered, and what was he doing on the beach in the wee small hours? This is looking like a scandal, Patricia. What are we going to do?'

'We? Nothing. It's got nothing to do with us. It's called, "Mind your own business".'

'Does Bobby know?'

'What do you think? He was the one who told me.'

Their conversation paused. The sisters faced a number of issues. Was the president murdered? If so, why and whodunit? What was he doing on the beach at night? And almost as important, who will be our new president, and what will be the impact on our Probus club?

Chapter 28
Evidence? What evidence?

The pathologist, referred to as Jock, looked skeptical which wasn't unusual; it was his default position. Dr Angus McAdam was a solid man with double brick skin. Born in Scotland, he grew up and studied in Glasgow and even after 20 odd years living Down Under, his accent could still cut through concrete. When Jock spoke, superfluous words were never a part of his lexicon. Why waste breath on unnecessary syllables? According to Jock, Stephen King nailed it with, "the road to hell is paved with adverbs."

He addressed DI Righteous. 'Tough task, laddie. You've got your work cut out with this one.' He pulled back the cotton cloth revealing Harry's head and chest. 'Waiting for blood results but nothing jumps out. Organs okay for a man his age. Minor bruising on chest but no significant marks on body. Seems his heart gave up.'

'What about his clothing, Doctor?' asked Richie, she of the "respect your elders society."

'No stains or apparent damage. Wallet intact, sans cash, handkerchief clean. A legal screed and something unusual.' He pointed to a bench. 'A wee white pebble in his right trouser pocket.'

'He was found with his trousers pulled down,' said Righteous. 'Any indication of sexual activity.'

'You're not listening, laddie. Nothing jumps out. When I hear back on the bloods I'll report. You may have better luck with forensics.'

The detectives nodded. 'Thanks,' said the DI and the officers left.

'Oh,' called the medico. 'Who the hell is Tommy Bent?'

The buzz amongst the good burghers of Brighton subsided to a bee-like hum. Patricia chatted with a few members before re-connecting with her sister.

'What have you heard?' she asked Jean.

'All gossip and guesswork,' replied baby sister. 'Bobby's our best and only source and even he knows nothing other than where the body was found and that homicide detectives are involved.'

'Are they saying it's murder?'

'Don't know and maybe even they don't know.'

'It must be connected to that body part found in his back yard.'

'Rear garden,' corrected Jean. 'Sorry? Do you think whoever murdered the victim at Harry's place has now done for the president?'

'Well if Harry participated in the owner of the missing limb meeting his death, this could be a simple case of revenge. You killed my mate, I'll kill you.'

Jean hit the brakes on the body on the beach subject. 'Do we need a special meeting to elect a new president?'

'How would I know?' replied Patricia oozing frustration. 'I'm not on the committee and when was the last time our sitting president was murdered mid-term?'

'There's no need to be sarcastic, Patricia.' The sarcasm was a clear sign someone had overstepped the mark. 'As vice-president, I assume Joan will automatically become president or acting president until our next AGM.'

Patricia drummed her fingers on the table. 'I'd better let my family know. They might be worried about me.'

'Okay. Bye,' said Jean and ended the call.

Some reacted badly to Harry's demise. Others fell out over it.

Margaret rang her brother, Terry. She still couldn't define her mood. Having been married to a man for nearly half a century, discovering he's now dead, and in unusual and/or suspicious circumstances, gives your body a decent old touch-up. The fact she wanted him dead made little difference. Her worry was that her brother or his criminal chums or both might be involved. Hello sinking feeling. The one bright spot was his body was found nowhere near their home, now, *her* home, all hers.

Thinking hurt. Her mind filled with thoughts of her brother, that musical trio of criminals and her reputation. It could be ruined. And was she guilty of conspiracy? If so, she could be off to the Dame Phyllis Frost holiday camp as a guest of King Charles the Third.

She rang her brother and spoke a strange language. Was her phone being tapped? Her recent visit to a police station pushed her worry beads to exhaustion.

'G'day Sis. Sorry to hear about big H.'

'Who told you?'

'Ah ... the talking wireless.'

'I need you to come here now.' The last word had order written all over it.

'Why?'

'Oh for God's sake, Terry. I've got a funeral to arrange, his paperwork to sort and a million other things to do. Why would you even ask? Now get here, soon as.'

She ended the call and Terry got the message. First he contacted the Murphy boys and started to sweat. Would Peter, Paul and Mary tell him if they knocked his brother-in-law last night in Brighton? They'd been told there was money in it if they did. Middle brother answered.

'Yeah?' said Paul, the thickest of the trio.

'It's me, Tel.'

'Wotcha want?'

'What did you guys get up to last night? Bit of a party, hey?'

Paul covered the phone badly and called. 'Pete?' he screamed.

'Wot?'

'Last night?'

'Wot about it?'

'Tel wants to know what we done?'

'He doesn't know? Is 'e havin' a laugh?'

Back to Terry went Paul. 'Pete wants to know is you havin' a laugh?'

'Did you lot have a meet with a bloke, the one who found that unusual thing in his rose garden?'

Peter yelled again. 'And tell him we is now owed that promised fee and the debt is growin' expo ... exponen ...'

If Peter couldn't pronounce exponentially, Paul had Buckley's. Paul started to speak but Terry heard what Peter said and felt sick.

'Okay,' was all Terry could muster and ended the call. 'Jesus,' he whispered,' and needed the loo.

He made it to Brighton a worried man. Big sister had pushed her grieving outside with the garbage. That was Harry's job and the lazy so-and-so had failed in his domestic duty. Once her brother was inside, she let fly.

'Why?' snapped Margaret. 'I told you to do nothing without my say so. If you've tied me in on this, you'll get nothing. Nothing! Oh and twenty years to life for murder.'

'I never killed no-one.'

Maybe not but the baby brother certainly copped a spray.

'At least this time you didn't bury him in the back yard,' she spat. Terry went to speak. 'Don't tell me. You said it y'self. What I don't know, I can't repeat.'

'Have the cops been?'

'Just to give me the good news. I'm sure the suits will be here later.'

She was desperate to ask him what happened but clamped her lips shut. Harry was dead and when she went to identify his body, there were no marks on his face and he kinda looked peaceful, almost happy. Whoever did for him, did a grand job.

'What do you want me to do?' asked Terry.

She paused before a sly grin started spreading across her face. 'Help me open a bottle of champers.'

Shocked and speechless, he looked at her and then the siblings laughed with a loud and throaty roar.

Chapter 29
The suspects

Cause of death was as yet unknown and the detectives knew Jock McAdam would never sign off unless he was certain. But if he declared the victim was murdered, the police needed to be ready. The circumstances of the body certainly pointed to homicide. Richie began building a case with names and photos covering two large display boards. She explained the details to the team.

'There was a legal letter in the deceased's pocket addressed to a Nixie Black.' Richie indicated the copy on the board. 'Apparently she's written a book about Sir Thomas Bent the former politician and developer, and the deceased's solicitor has threatened or warned Nixie about publishing.'

'Why?' asked a member of the team.

'From the letter it seems Harry believed he'd be libelled in the unpublished book. How? No idea.'

'We'll need to interview this woman and obtain a copy of her book,' said the DI.

'What's the significance of the Tommy Bent homemade sign found on the body?' asked a Senior Constable.

Richie pointed to a photo of the sign. 'No idea but a volunteer is needed to check on this and on Mr Bent.' The look from Richie saw the word volunteer lose its meaning.

'Me and my big mouth,' said the Senior Constable as the others laughed.

Richie continued and pointed to a police photo from Harry Penshurst's rear garden. 'Recently there was a human body part, a severed arm, no hand, discovered in the victim's back garden buried beneath some blood red roses. Recently, uniform arrested a local crim for nicking a new BMW. On the thief's mobile was the number of our victim's brother-in-law.'

Senior Constable Damien Bramble was curious. 'Say that again. Our victim has just had part of a corpse buried in his garden? Why weren't we investigating that and surely there's a connection.'

'A single limb with the rest of the body missing does not necessarily a homicide make, Damien, but your contribution is duly noted,' said Richie.

The SIO took control. 'Thanks Richie,' he said. 'And we are consulting with the DI working on the body part case. Now, anything else?'

'We're working on the victim's background, assets, finances and will,' replied Richie. 'All we really need is Dr McAdam's decision that the body on Brighton beach is a homicide.'

'Right,' said the DI. 'Let's proceed with caution under the assumption the victim was murdered.'

'I've never known a suicide to hide in bushes, lose their strides and bung a sign around their neck,' said Bramble. 'And have no obvious signs of injury.'

'Agreed, it's odds on a murder,' said the DI. 'There are interviews, places to go, people to see. I'll check with forensics and Jock. Richie will set the field for the rest of you. Bramble, you're at silly point. Happy?'

Bramble went looking for his helmet and box as officers nodded, agreed, and started work.

Righteous and Richie pulled up outside the Penshurst property. Margaret, dressed in black, let them in. She owned three black hats and wondered if the one with a black veil was too much for the funeral.

Introductions were made. 'May we start, madam,' said the DI, 'by offering our condolences on the loss of your husband.'

'Thank you,' she said trying to look and behave as an innocent, recently bereaved widow. 'Can I offer you coffee?'

'Thank you, no,' said the DI and they sat in the main sitting room which could have doubled as an upmarket furniture retailer's showroom.

Margaret decided to take control. 'You said you're homicide detectives. My limited knowledge of the police gleaned from watching TV, tells me you investigate murders. So how did my husband die?'

'We're still waiting for the forensic pathologist to make his finding, Mrs Penshurst, and of course we'll keep you informed of any developments.'

'If you don't know the cause of death, it may not be a homicide. And anyway, I can't bury my husband unless you release his body. This is the most stressful time of my life and you're making it worse. Why the delay?'

'We understand your difficulty but there are laws which require a death certificate to be completed and until the cause of death is known, there will be what we hope is only a minor hold up.'

'Are you saying he died a natural death?'

'That's for the forensic pathologist to determine. There were some unusual events surrounding his death and ...'

'Unusual? What do you mean by unusual?'

Margaret was gently raising the temperature and Righteous wisely gave his female colleague an imperceptible, to the widow, nod.

'Did your husband often walk to the beach at Brighton, Mrs Penshurst?'

'Yes he did.'

'In the middle of the night?'

It worked. A female asking pointed questions knocked Margaret off her perch. The widow paused.

'No, always during the day.'

'Can you take us through your last 24 hours? When did you last see your husband?'

The pendulum swung and the detectives were running the interview.

'We had dinner then Harry went out about 7.30, probably to his club.'

'You don't know where he went?'

Margaret's dander stood up. 'My husband often went out and is not required to sign the hotel register.' Richie paused giving Margaret more rope.

'He wasn't home when I went to bed at 10. I woke at about 7 this morning, couldn't find him and that's when I started looking.'

'Did you get up during the night?'

'I did,' said Margaret and left it there. The police were waiting for her to continue. She hated having to do so. 'My husband and I have separate bedrooms, both ensuite.'

Righteous took over. 'Do you know of any problems your husband had? Business disputes, strained relationships, that sort of thing?'

Margaret couldn't stop herself. 'What, now you're saying he had a mistress or took his own life?'

'We're saying nothing of the sort, Mrs Penshurst. He may have died of natural causes or he may have been the victim of foul play. But if you know about something troubling him, for example financial worries, it could be helpful and assist in our investigation.'

'Nothing. He was angry about the business of the bone buried in the garden but as he had nothing to do with it, he dismissed it.'

'We've had reports your brother is familiar with criminals.'

'Oh for God's sake. My brother smokes a bit of weed. Is that the best you can do?' Her guts began dancing. Could she disguise her panic?

Righteous needed a backup and Richie took control.

'Did your husband have any business dealings which may have been unsuccessful and made him an enemy ... or two.'

Excellent question especially as the DS had done her research and found court documents on the Carter Thomas verses Henry Penshurst case. Margaret was torpedoed below the water line causing her anger to fizzle. In another country's jurisdiction, she pleaded the Fifth.

'I was never involved in my husband's business affairs.' Her ability to lie and lie convincingly collapsed, and Richie went for the kill.

'Have you heard of a man, Carter Thomas?'

The widow shook her head scrambling for an answer. 'Doesn't ring a bell. Sorry.'

'He sued your husband over a business deal that went sour.'

'If you say so.'

'Mr Thomas lost twice being ordered to pay your husband's costs.'

She shrugged. 'Can't help you,' she said glaring at the female detective and if looks could kill, Margaret committed murder in her own home.

DI Righteous had heard enough and stood. 'Thank you for your time, Mrs Penshurst. Again our condolences on your loss.'

Once the front door closed, the ungrieving widow let fly, reciting the entire first page of *Cursing for Angry People*.

Back in their car, the detectives agreed. Margaret Penshurst couldn't lie straight in bed, separate rooms or not.

Chapter 30

The three amigos

Patricia collected her sister and they drove to Bobby's place. 'And he *invited* us?' asked Jean. 'You didn't pressure him?'

'Let's not fall out again, Jean. I'm not a pushy person,' said Patricia.

'I beg to differ.'

'How can we investigate Harry's death if we're going to squabble over something so trivial?'

'The police investigate. We observe, comment and gossip.'

'Look, Bobby has contacts in the police. They give him information and he passes it on to us. It's obvious he wants to get involved even from the sidelines, and we are his sounding board. He wants us to give him feedback on his theories about who killed our beloved president.'

'It's ex-president and nobody, not one living soul loved him.'

'God rest his soul,' said atheist Patricia.

'Harry Penshurst and *soul* do not belong in the same sentence.'

Bobby let them in, they chatted with Glenda who looked pretty in lilac before Harry led the cohorts to his study.

'Ladies,' he said when all were seated. 'I'll be frank.'

Jean couldn't resist. 'If you're Frank, bags be Ernest.'

Patricia wanted to slap her sister but Bobby laughed so hard she forced a smile. He continued.

'Because we all knew Harry, because he's been our Probus president for so long, and did so much for the club, I've got a special interest in seeing his killer or killers brought to justice. Of course the police will investigate but we know stuff which might help them.'

Patricia wanted to ask, 'What stuff?' but let the former cop continue.

'If the detectives miss something, or don't arrest anyone for lack of evidence, or if there is somebody who knows something but won't talk, maybe we can help.'

The sisters were excited.

'The main question is did Harry die of natural causes or was he murdered?'

'What do the police say?' asked Patricia.

'What do *you* say?' asked Jean.

Bobby hesitated. 'Well he may have had a heart attack, but what was he doing in the undergrowth behind the bathing boxes in the wee small hours, with a sign on his chest listing the words, *Harry Bent*, and with his trousers pulled down?'

The sisters gasped. Blood, disembowelment, and decapitation they could manage but Harry sans strides made them shudder. It was the stuff of nightmares.

Jean was now into the swing of her new career. 'What can we do? How can I help?'

Bobby had been thinking about this meeting. 'How about we make a list of people who had dealings with Harry and any events in which he was involved. If we're not sure of anything or reckon we need more details, we consult with one another. Once our list is complete we can plan.'

'Draw up our strategies,' added Patricia.

Bobby pointed at her. 'Clever girl,' he said then died thinking the word *girl* was sexist or demeaning or just plain wrong.

Jean jumped in. 'We're more than happy to be your girls, Officer.'

Patricia agreed, Bobby felt better and everyone grinned. The three amigos were off and running.

'Oh, there's one other thing,' said Bobby. 'Do you think we should have a name for our group?'

'What, like *The Famous Five*?' suggested Jean.

Patricia wanted to die. She last read Enid Blyton 61 years ago.

'I was thinking more of something like PUDA,' said the retired policeman. The sisters stared, confused. 'Yes, it's an acronym for the Probus Unofficial Detective Agency.'

Thanks to Lewis Carroll, the sisters imitated that Cheshire cat.

Chapter 31
Jock's diagnosis

The good police medico, Angus "Jock" McAdam, had worked on some extraordinary corpses in his work history. The Barlinnie is a Glasgow prison, the biggest in Scotland, and known as The Big Hoose. It's where the prisoners take no prisoners and for Jock, examining grotesque wounds of a crim who copped a jail sentence with the added bonus of a jolly good kicking, stabbing, or strangling was no job for the squeamish. A couple of prisoners working as lackeys to the good doc were not so butch and brave after all. They would throw up, faint and even run screaming from the autopsy while the hardy pathologist probed and picked his way through intestines, eye sockets, and genitalia.

And all that contrasts with the examination of Henry Fitzgibbon Leigh Penshurst. Of blood and guts were there none. The body posed a powerful challenge to the Glaswegian. No corpse unpicked was wee Jock's mantra although the man was no more wee than he was a Sassenach.

Harry's autopsy took time. The world waited for Jock's verdict. It was the jury refusing to leave the jury room. Tension grew. For Jock, Harry's bloods were normal apart from tiny traces of something common. Alcohol was well represented but the man could hold his whisky and Class A drugs were a foreign language to the old-school horrible Harry.

Finally Jock nailed it. Harry was a dog. Well, he'd been called far worse. No, by dog, he was not a scab, snitch, or scallywag. He was put down as a veterinarian would a hound. Make him drowsy then when pliable, up the anaesthetic and bingo, heart stops. Simple as.

But how was the drug administered and where? What part or parts of the body served as the entry point? Damn good questions which is why the death certificate took so long to be signed.

DI Righteous took the call. When he heard the news, he slapped his desk and team members outside his office paid attention.

'Thank you, Jock. You are a gentleman and a scholar.' Righteous addressed the squad members.

'Ladies and gentlemen, Dr McAdam has signed the death certificate and officially, we have a homicide. Harry Penshurst was murdered.'

How ironic that Harry ingested what millions absorb every day. A trip to the dentist, medical procedures, even skin cancers removed by your GP in their rooms. Local or general, anaesthetics are given everywhere. Sick or injured pets are "put to sleep" enabling them to cross the rainbow bridge.

Jock was convinced this was what did for his patient although not completely. It was as if someone had sat on him and literally squeezed him to death, an easy task with the anaesthetic coursing through his veins.

Mind you the pathologist was putting his reputation on the line. He knew if it came to a trial, he would be called and the defence would bring in their own specialist who would challenge Jock's diagnosis. Juries don't like expert witnesses fighting a duel at 10 paces. Confusion produces dissent and "beyond reasonable doubt" grows legs.

Jock decided Harry died when a hypodermic penetrated his overweight body and sent an anaesthetic into his bloodstream.

The killer or killers were clever. If Margaret Penshurst was correct in saying Harry went out at 7.30pm and he was murdered within say an hour or two and his body hidden and not found for say 10 hours, the ingested material had time to fade from view, possibly disappear altogether.

Some rapists use drugs to render their victim helpless. Not that Harry was ever a rapist as he relied on his pure false charm to seduce women. But someone decided to do the bastard in by sticking a needle into his unattractive body and lull him to unconsciousness and thus to death.

But whereabouts in the president's body did the drug enter? Harry's flesh, as creepy as it was to some people, many people, was not riddled with pin holes from drug taking. Therefore jabbing the victim on his arm or thigh would be easy to discover. But this murderer or these murderers did well. Were they medicos?

Crinkly skin of a senior ain't perfect and it's certainly not the skin of a baby's bottom. A senior person watches their body wrinkle and age with time. Harry aged badly. It took some magnificent magnification for Jock to pull off the autopsy of the year. Harry's case was a homicide.

For the police, the game was afoot.

Chapter 32
The gang of four

Nixie had spent an age reading and re-reading her letter from Harry's solicitor. Her guts burned with anger. Her blood, sweat and tears were sacrificed to research and write her book. She visited Tommy Bent's grave and statue, took photos, and wrote with passion. When cousin Michael Blackmore arrived on the scene and gave her such detailed family history, her book took on a new angle.

She found a book designer who produced what the author reckoned to be a brilliant cover. More honing of the text, and publishing D-Day drew ever closer.

But that damn legal letter tossed a massive spanner in the works making her miserable then angry then furious. She studied her options and the most attractive by a long chalk was to murder Harry Penshurst. Of course being sensible, she knew she would almost certainly get caught but that didn't stop her considering the possibility.

Okay, if not murder, then how could she remove the legal threat to publication?

Things took an unexpected but exciting change when she met Naomi Carruthers in the carpark of the building where the Brighton Probus club held their meetings. Naomi explained Lionel's tale of woe.

'That makes perfect sense,' said the author. 'Penshurst doesn't care about anyone except himself. He needs to be stopped. Agreed?'

Naomi didn't hesitate. 'Agreed.'

'Right, so what can we do?

'What would you like to see happen?'

'Remove any legal action against my book. What about you?'

'Expose his devious scheme to cheat his way to a public award.'

'Okay, sounds good but how?'

'We get him in a private place, make sure he's helpless, then take photos which will embarrass him into silence. He will become a recluse, frightened to show his face in public. Bullies hate being ridiculed.'

'Blackmail,' said Nixie rubbing her hands with glee. 'I love it but as I said, how?'

'I'm working on it. I told you there are others who want to stop Penshurst. They share our passion to puncture the pompous prick. When the plan is set, I'll be in touch.'

Naomi and Carter became the team leaders. Carter kept Spiteri in the dark knowing he could become extremely angry at the slightest provocation, and collaborating with women would terrify or infuriate him. Naomi gave Nixie bare details. This is the plan the leaders chose.

Carter and Spiteri would kidnap and rob Harry then pass the hapless victim to the ladies who would photograph the brute. No-one is killed, the males receive funds and the females obtain compromising photos. Penshurst will be terrified to report the attack to the police.

Harry's enemies became the gang of four, a quartet of highly-motivated warriors. All had different reasons to attack the president, separate roles to play and goals to achieve and in partnership, they were eager to strike.

The plot took shape with the day, time and venue chosen. Harry would be kidnapped, robbed, then delivered to the beach at Brighton where the women would prepare him for a photo session. Carter and Spiteri were to hold down the villain as the women administered a drug. Once sleepy, the chaps would vanish leaving the gals to place a sign on Harry and take his "Say cheese!" photos leaving the president to be found muddled and embarrassed. Ah, but would the plan work? Naomi worried. She kept hearing a line of poetry. "The best laid schemes o' mice an' men. Gang aft a-gley."

Two days after Harry was found dead, reclining under bushes at Brighton beach, Nixie heard her door bell. It was an old ring pull rarely seen except in ancient abodes. Nixie's place was old and matched her attire—unusual.

She opened the door and felt ill. Here stood the Homicide detectives, Righteous and Richie. They planned to concentrate on that legal letter and Richie opened the bowling.

'Ms Black, may I call you Nixie, it's such an unusual name.'

'Okay,' said the author. 'What's this all about?'

She looked nervous, fidgeting and squinting, pushing her specs with their striped, orange frames, up and down her Jimmy Durante schnoz.

'Nixie, we're investigating the death of Mr Harry Penshurst. Do you know the gentleman?'

'Not personally.'

'You've never met him?'

'I just said that.'

'You've never had any dealings with him?'

'Not with him personally.' Her unconvincing lies kept multiplying.

'Not with any of his business associates?'

That one was too hard to push aside. 'His solicitor sent me a registered letter about a book I'm writing.'

Thanks to the victim's pockets, the police acquired said letter and were in a strong position to ask their next question. The DI left everything to Richie. She was good and especially so when interviewing females.

'This letter, what was it about?'

Nixie took a deep breath and tried to make the subject as trivial as possible. 'Mr Penshurst was interested in the subject of my book, the late politician, Sir Thomas Bent.'

Richie slipped into her surprised detective role. 'His solicitor sent a registered letter to express his interest in your book? Why a registered letter?'

Nixie kept stalling and digging, the hole getting deeper. She gave in. 'He believed I would publish material which would cast Mr Penshurst in a bad light.'

'And you wanted to stop him taking legal action?'

'Yes, *no!*' she quickly changed her plea. Just as she seemed to crumble, the DI swooped in for the kill.

'Where were you last night from 7pm onwards?'

'What?'

'It's a simple question, Nixie,' said Richie.

'I was here, at home, working on my manuscript.'

'All night?' asked the DI.

'Yes.'

'Can anyone verify that?'

'No, *yes!* Both Rousseau and Stravinsky were with me the whole time.' She paused. 'They're my cats and would never lie.'

'May we have a sample of your handwriting, Ms Black?' asked Righteous. 'Printing actually.'

Richie handed her an A4 pad and marker pen, 'Two words please, Nixie, in block letters. *Tommy Bent.*'

This was super uncomfortable for the homeowner and Stravinsky moved forward head butting his mistress's leg as if to say, 'Don't let them bully you, Mummy.'

Nixie hesitated then obliged. For a second she thought about writing with her left hand but could see the police didn't come down in the last shower. She printed then handed back the pad and pen. Both detectives gave the art work a cursory glance. A detailed study awaited.

They thanked the cat lady and left.

That night, her cats couldn't settle on their bed, in reality Nixie's, because she found sleep nigh on impossible. Tossing and turning upset the moggies. Nixie wanted to stop Harry Penshurst and the cops regarded her most definitely as a person of interest.

Chapter 33

Probus in session

It was the first Probus meeting since that tragic event. Of course everyone knew he was dead. It was all over the TV news. Everyone had spoken to someone about the events. A few tried to speak to everyone.

Members arrived and greetings were sombre. No hugs or hearty handshakes. One notable absentee was the late president's better half.

The bell on the front table rang as if with cloth draped over it, a muffled bell, and people took their seats. The third seat on the left aisle was noticeably vacant. People spotted the situation and felt extra sympathy for the new widow.

Joan took the microphone. 'Good morning everyone.'

The response from the packed room was gentle. 'Good morning.'

'Thank you for your attendance today on what is a very sad occasion for our Probus club. You were as shocked as I when we heard our dear president had died.'

'Hear, hear,' came from a few members.

'Yesterday I spoke with Margaret and she has been overwhelmed with the cards, letters, and emails you have sent expressing your condolences. I asked about funeral arrangements and she said something I found distressing. The police are unsure as to the cause of Harry's death hence the delay in releasing his body.'

A murmur arose. Many, no, most members had been speculating about the circumstances of his passing. Since his death, questions raced through the air with digital phones and emails working overtime.'

'What was he doing out in the wee small hours?'

'Did he have a heart attack?'

'What are the police not telling us?'

Joan continued. 'There are some housekeeping matters we need to deal with. I will be acting president until our annual general meeting when all positions will be declared vacant. As always we encourage everyone to consider joining the committee. Our club is as strong as our volunteers.

'Talking with committee members this past week, we decided to ask today's speaker to reschedule and instead throw the floor open to anyone who wanted to tell their favourite memory or memories of Harry. He was a special person and I know many of you have told me you wish to speak.'

Another murmur broke out and this unusual monthly meeting had the potential to go either way. The list of members having a birthday was read with best wishes being showered on all.

The members telling their favourite Harry anecdote provoked laughs. A few members didn't laugh aloud. Some didn't even smile. They all knew one must never speak ill of the dead so kept their true feelings under wraps.

Over a cuppa, people mingled and the two sleuthing sisters finished either side of Bobby[2].

The usual greeting and shared family news was soon over and the retired senior constable lowered his voice. The sisters leant in, hooked.

'I've just heard from my mate in the force. The pathologist has decided.' He paused, not deliberately, then whispered his next sentence. 'Harry Penshurst was murdered.'

The sisters reacted in such a way that a few people stopped talking and turned to see what had happened.

The three amigos sat there stunned at being stared at. Patricia broke the freeze frame. 'Let me get you a cuppa, Senior,' she said and headed off to the kitchen.

Jean asked after Glenda but soon switched to another topic. It's not hard to guess what that was.

Chapter 34
We all want the money

Margaret despaired. Her husband was deceased. Great. But how he died and who killed him was unknown to her. Unknown to most people including the police. She wanted access to Harry's Fort Knox strong box. But financial institutions are successful because they stick to extremely strict rules. In this case, no death certificate, no access. I mean how many relatives bump off their family member desperate to grab grandpa or grandma's life insurance?

The widow burned with rage at the bloody police asking more questions and giving nothing in return. How long would this drag on?

But if she thought that was bad, worse, far worse lurked in the shadows. The business with the buried body part just wouldn't go away. It loomed as the key to Harry's homicide. Terry's criminal chums killed a druggie who failed to repay his debt. The crims gave Terry the body part which he buried in Harry's garden.

It was hidden beneath those blood red roses with which Harry once won first prize in a horticultural show. True. There was a rumour the judges were nobbled but nothing was ever proved.

Now, oh God no, please no!—Terry's mates, having been told his sister wanted her hubby to become fish food, were inspired to actually do the deed. Or did they?

Okay, to be fair, if the Murphy trio did assassinate Terry's brother-in-law and thus were entitled to a huge payout, they did the deed with finesse. Not the usual style of Peter, Paul, and Mary. The weasel Willims, without an *a*, looked like a soldier in the Bosworth Field with axe marks, arrows through his head and a slice from a sword the size of a pikestaff to finish him off. A relatively small part of him ended up in a Brighton backyard, no, rear garden. Poor chap. On the other hand, Harry was discovered whole and almost pristine.

How come?

And not only was there no bashing, stabbing, or shooting to off Harry—clever—there lay the Probus big wig sans strides, tackle in the front window and wearing a *Tommy Bent* sign on his chest. Why put him in a strange place—the undergrowth behind the bathing boxes? Oh, and the corpse was smiling. Was he done over while out playing silly buggers with someone offering their favours for a fee? This did not have the mark of the minor league mafia from North Frankston.

But if Peter, Paul, and Mary did do the deed thanks to her dopey brother, it could all come screaming back to Margaret. She'd get no dough, acquire a black widow's reputation, and spend years in a prison cell.

Think of that horrendous jailbird clobber. No haute couture in there, darling.

She was afraid to ask Terry what might have happened. Surely any phone calls could and would be traced. Emails were worse. Technical gurus could find any deleted text. She felt desperation closing in.

Mind you, things were equally grim with her only living relative. Brother Terry used the trio of Peter, Paul, and Mary for weed. He got his own supply from them and did a spot of dealing for beer money.

When big sis told him she wanted Harry to hurry up and die a natural death, Terry got thinking. He wallowed in inspiration once his sister offered to financially reward him should he fulfil her dream. When Terry heard the folk-singing trio were about to knock a minor league dog for non-payment of drug fees, he asked for a body part with a promise of big bucks on any future projects. He briefly mentioned his brother-in-law being loaded, reminding the lads about the theory of the redistribution of wealth where the cash and assets of the rich should be spread amongst those what are broke, like.

Now Terry panicked. Harry Penshurst *was* dead, literally, actually, and the trio wanted their whack. And Terry certainly knew what the lads did to anyone who stiffed them their share. Don't pay, you sail away. And worse, Terry couldn't swim.

What a predicament. Visit the trio and have his favourite digit removed and presented to him as a reminder to cough up, or to lie low and hope they give him more time.

His sister didn't contact him and that could only be bad. Obviously, she was unable to access hubby's stash. Of course once she could, he'd cop his cabbage and be able to remove the death sentence the Murphy siblings would soon put out on him.

Siblings, Margaret and Terry, wallowed in pain, mental torture of the worst kind. Alas it was about to get even worse.

Superannuation is big business. Companies daily manage massive amounts of money where the top executives earn enough to buy watches worth what their underlings make in a year. With such funds involved, security needs to be state of the art. There are whole departments employed to keep the company's assets safe.

The best attempts to steal are clever. When someone tries a basic spot of fraud, they're easily discovered and denied. A security officer at Harry Penshurst's super fund company, noticed some attempts at remote access.

The would-be fraudster used the right access code but placed it in the wrong box. Fail. Try again. This happened a lot when the stake holder's memory needed a refill, or by drinking late at night, resulting in their fingers stabbing the wrong keys.

Poor old Margaret couldn't take a trick. She'd tried and failed and now Harry's account was listed as one to watch for possible fraud.

Chapter 35
Cops get busy

The homicide team assigned to the case reviewed the situation. DI Righteous addressed the troops.

'Right, the good Scottish doctor has given his meticulously prepared verdict of homicide, with his death certificate giving the cause as pressure on the chest together with the ingesting, would you believe, of anaesthetic. So, next we chat with persons of interest, collect evidence, and, hopefully, make arrests.'

Senior Constable Damien Bramble was the inquisitive kind. 'Question, boss. How many murder victims do we know who, just before they're killed, have a human body part discovered in their rose garden? The two things just have to be connected.'

'It's called stating the bleeding obvious, Damien,' said Richie who was good at calling a spade a bloody shovel. She moved to the board, pointed to different photos and exhibits as she spoke. 'Murder victim, wife, brother of wife, connected to three brothers well-known county lines drug runners with Class B their speciality.'

'County lines?' asked a confused Bramble. 'We're not in the UK, sarge.'

'Frankston to Rosebud,' explained Richie and the room erupted.

Righteous took over. 'So, does the wife tell her brother to have his drug buddies knock her husband? Why would the wife want her spouse killed? What's the connection between any of this coterie and the buried human limb? For mine, where we stand, as so many folk today say, at this point in time, no magistrate will sign a search warrant for anything based on our shaky or rather, very shaky evidence.'

Richie pointed to a photo and a letter. 'Another leading candidate is Nixie Black, J D Vance's favourite cat lady, and author of a self-published book about Tommy Bent. Ms Black received a letter from Harry's solicitor, found on the victim's body, threatening her against libelling his client. She would benefit from Harry's death and Ms Black, apart from her cats swearing on a tin of Whiska's she was home at the time, has no alibi for the night of the murder.'

'And what's the significance of the sign on the victim's chest – *Harry Bent*?' asked the DI. 'That certainly suggests the wonderful Nixie.'

'What do we know about the widow and the marriage?' asked Bramble.

'She has no alibi for the night and the couple had been married for about 50 years,' said Richie.

'Fifty years,' said someone. The whole squad joined in the gag. 'You get less for murder!'

Richie kept going and pointed to a photo. 'Our third suspect is Carter Thomas, former business associate of the victim and a truly angry man. Carter and Harry fell out over a land development scheme. Carter lost big money, sued Harry, lost and lost again when ordered to pay the defendant's costs.'

'Full points for motive,' said someone.

Richie stepped back for her boss. 'So known suspects are one, the group of widow, brother-in-law, and his criminal mates, two, the historical author and three, a former business partner. Comments?'

Bramble raised what he thought was an interesting point. 'Has their local Probus club got anything to do with his death?'

'Explain,' said the DI.

'Well he was their president and there are about a hundred members. If only 1% believe in presidential assassination or regicide, we could have our killer.'

The laughter and cat-calling needed to be stopped by the DI.

'Thank you, Senior. Have you thought about a career change? Improbable murder mysteries might be right up your street.'

'A dead end street,' called someone and the hilarity resumed.

As the police joked, the three amigos, the Probus Unofficial Detective Agency or PUDA members, as they were now calling themselves, got stuck into their first official meeting.

'Let's not get ahead of ourselves, ladies,' said Bobby. 'We're here to help the professionals and discreetly at that. I don't want us to become the real detectives. The police are the main characters and we, if anything, are the bit players.'

'The walking wallpaper,' suggested Patricia.

'Exactly, well said, Grannie Number 1,' smiled Bobby and both women laughed. They lapped up his every word. 'I'll get details from my mate, the one still a serving officer, and if we reckon there's something the police might miss or have missed, I can return serve and hope it helps get the result we all want.'

'Should we keep minutes?' asked Jean, serious and keen.

Bobby looked at Patricia. She gave a small nod and Jean whipped out a pad and pen from her bag. Her long ago career as a shorthand typist resumed.

'What do we know about the pathology report? asked Patricia.

'It seems as if he was drugged.'

'Drugged!' exclaimed the sisters as one.

'To me that's not a brutal killer but someone calm, collected and determined,' said Bobby.

'Who do the police suspect?' asked Jean.

Bobby shook his head. 'I won't be told crucial details like that. What I'm told I'll pass to you ladies. I'll have a theory or two and will need you to check my ideas and provide feedback. What do you say?'

Patricia began. 'We regard helping you, Senior Constable Ayers, open brackets, Retired, close brackets, as a privilege and a pleasure. We're in your hands, Skipper.'

'What she said,' added Jean.

'Not literally I hope,' he replied and the sisters' smiles lit up the room.

Chapter 36
The after effects of crime

Lionel Carruthers wanted out of Probus. His shock and disappointment at discovering his so-called friend, the late Harry Penshurst, had deceived him, continued to dog his thinking. His mental health report read *Needs watching*. Not that there was a medical examination but had there been, serious action might have been ordered.

Depression can be debilitating and dangerous.

His wife saw the effect on her husband and developed a hatred for the pompous president. She put her wrath to one side wanting her older husband to find a way out of his misery. And, of course, she had found a new friend who too had a reason to dislike, no, hate Harry Penshurst. Were these two women involved in the death of the Probus president?

'I'm finished with Probus,' said Lionel. 'I never want to go back to that place again.'

'No, Lionel,' argued Naomi. 'Apart from the disgraceful behaviour of that man, now dead, you've loved every minute of your time there. You told me the trip to Bright was wonderful, and especially your visit to the old Bright railway station and its goods shed. You showed me the photos you took.'

'Yes, yes, it was really interesting.'

'You've told me several times the guest speakers at Probus have taught you so much, and some of the friends you've made and now spend time with outside of Probus, give you a reason to get up in the morning.'

He nodded and tried but failed to smile. 'It's true,' he said. 'You're probably right and that man is no longer around to lie to me ever again.'

'And being the treasurer means all your accountancy experience is being put to a new and worthwhile use. Stick with it, Lionel. Forget that sick and evil man, I won't even say his name, and become an important person in your club.'

'Thank you, my dear. I'll think about it.' Naomi kissed him then went to make their tea while he returned to an article he was writing for his favourite railway journal.

Jean wrote up the minutes of the PUDA meeting and sent them to Patricia by email asking for comments. Big sister was favourably impressed and said so. No sooner had she sent the email than her front doorbell sounded.

On her doorstep was her favourite granddaughter, Vicky, with a young man Grannie didn't know.

'Hello Gran.'

'Hello my darling.'

'This is my boyfriend, Gavin.'

She greeted the probable future member of her new and extended family. They sat in the lounge while Patricia fussed in the kitchen. She glowed inside knowing her granddaughter wanted to introduce her beau to Gran.

She called. 'Now is it tea or coffee, Gavin?'

'Coffee.' He didn't know what to call Patricia or how to say please.

'And tea for you, Vicky.'

'Yes please, Gran.'

Gavin spoke to his girlfriend. 'You drink coffee. You told me that.'

'No I don't. Well sometimes but mostly it's tea.'

He looked at her and frowned. She pointed to some framed photos of Patricia and Jean. 'People say I look like Gran when she was young.'

Gavin looked and shook his head. 'I don't see it.'

Patricia arrived with a plate of biscuits and a bowl of mixed nuts. 'Help yourself please.'

'How have you been keeping, Gran?' asked Vicky.

'I'm well thank you, darling, but my sister and I have had some shocking news this week. It's terrible actually. The president of our Probus club has been murdered.'

The young visitors reacted.

'Mum told me,' said Vicky.

'Was that the body on the beach?' asked Gavin.

'Yes. The police have released few details. We have a retired police officer in the Probus club and Jean and I are trying to help him help the Homicide detectives.'

'What, you mean Grannie power?' mocked Gavin. 'The pensioner police!'

Vicky gave him a mild slap and a gentle rebuke. 'Gavin, don't be rude.'

The kettle boiled and Patricia left to return with the beverages. 'Help yourself to milk and sugar,' she said then sat back and observed her male visitor. In old-fashioned terms, she didn't like the cut of his jib.

'So what do you do, Gavin? Are you a student?'

'Nah, motor mechanic. I work for the old man.'

'He's very good, Gran. Gavin could look after your Mazda and have it running like new.'

'Excellent. So my grandson who's a GP can offer advice about my aching bones, and my granddaughter's boyfriend can service my car. I've fallen on my feet with this new family.'

The females smiled. The male didn't. For him, there was no such thing as mates' rates, and especially not for wealthy old women.

They chatted and Patricia grew more uncomfortable. Of course she would never criticize her guest and she worried, being brand new to this family lark, if she should say or do anything about her feelings.

This young man is not suitable for my granddaughter.

Chapter 37
Find the murderer

Once Jock McAdam signed the death certificate describing Harry's death as a homicide, the hunt for his killer was on in earnest. DI Righteous continued addressing the troops.

'If I thought we had a single suspect or even a decent person of interest, I'd say. I've got a feeling in my water there's a conspiracy in this case. No sudden attack by a stranger. No shot in the dark, literally, but something planned and deliberate.'

'Well it would have to be planned, boss, if it was deliberate,' said Detective Senior Constable Bramble, the pedant of the squad.

Others looked at him and sighed or groaned.

'Any favourite, Senior?' asked the boss.

'I still think there's a connection between the murder on the beach and the hacked limb in his garden. Crack the burial in the rose garden and you'll have the killer of Harry Penshurst.'

Righteous looked at his team. 'Any more for any more?'

No-one wanted to stick out their neck. Stating their belief or theory in public, well amongst the other detectives, left one open to a fall if wrong.

'Cowards,' said Righteous and gave out tasks. He and DS Benaud would interview Carter Thomas but a phone call delayed their departure. Righteous answered. It finished and he spoke with the team member managing the finances of the victim. 'You notified all banks and super funds with whom he has funds. Had them freeze everything.'

'Once we knew he was dead, all done, boss.' Righteous appreciated the quality of his fellow detectives.

He and Benaud walked to their car.

'That was a security guy from one of the banks where Harry Penshurst does business. The night he was killed, the dead man made several withdrawals of the maximum amount possible. Freezing his accounts was too late.'

'Much taken?'

'Yes,' said Righteous, 'well, the maximum allowed and from all his accounts. He had several.' The DI tossed the keys to Richie.

They discussed Carter Thomas en route to his home address. 'If it comes to motive,' said Righteous, 'this man's at the front of the queue. He lost a major moolah over one of Penshurst's development schemes. Carter sued him and lost, and lost again having to pay the defendant's costs.'

'How do you want to manage him?' asked Richie.

'Soft and gentle. He'll be the type who planned his revenge. Remember Shakespeare told us it's a dish best served cold.'

'I think you're wrong, sir.'

'What? You reckon revenge should be enacted as soon as possible?'

'No, your attribution. Forget the Bard, I know it comes from a novel by a Frenchman, a boy called Sue.'

The DI looked at her thinking again about his assessment. This DS was one smart cookie. She reinforced his opinion with her next remark.

'Did you know, sir, our suspect's address is in Bentleigh, a suburb named after Thomas Bent, whose name was prominently displayed on the victim's chest?'

'Thank you, I did know that but as to its relevance in this case I know nussing,' he said with a Sergeant Schultz from *Hogan's Heroes* accent.

Richie was used to her boss and his pathetic impersonations, and made small talk until they reached Carter's abode. There were no pebbles on the gate post at the front of his property.

The detectives knocked on the front door and Mrs Thomas opened it. After introductions, the lady of the house whacked their opening delivery for six.

'I'm sorry, you've just missed him. Carter's gone fishing and won't be back for a few days. Can I help you with anything?'

'Where has he gone, Mrs Thomas?'

'Oh somewhere down in the Gippsland Lakes. What's this about? He's not in any trouble is he?'

The police were used to this situation. To explain or to say nothing. If Carter participated in the death of Harry Penshurst, he wouldn't need to be a genius to figure out homicide detectives would likely come calling. The person of interest had been thinking ahead, and in this instance the detectives chose to say nowt.

'I could give you his mobile number but reception out on the water is as good as useless.'

'We'll pop back, madam. Good day,' said Righteous and the couple left.

As they walked down the drive, Richie stopped causing her DI to do likewise.

'What's up?' he asked.

She pointed to the middle of the driveway and Righteous twigged. He reckoned this woman would win promotion sooner rather than later.

Carter Thomas had hundreds of little white pebbles decorating the centrepiece of his driveway. Harry Penshurst had a little white pebble in the pocket of his pulled-down pants when found deceased at the rear of the Brighton bathing boxes.

'It would be nice if some of Carter's DNA could be found on Harry's pebble,' said the boss and they left.

In the car, Richie observed. 'The wife must have known her husband's nemesis was recently murdered. If so, she was acting nice and cool. And how could they own that house having lost a pile of cash?'

'Might be in her name,' replied Righteous. 'Tell me, Detective Sergeant, what's the first thing you would do if you've just murdered a rival and relieved him of his readies?'

'Leave town.'

'And go somewhere isolated where phone coverage is non-existent.'

'Should we have asked to see his passport?' asked Richie.

'Perhaps but tell me. Could one man have captured Penshurst, controlled him, drugged him, fleeced him of his cash, and transported the corpulent carcass to the beach at Brighton and done him in?'

'Carter must be a flexible giant, sir,' she said.

'Or else?'

'He had an accomplice.'

'Or accomplices plural. So how will we locate such a person or persons?'

'I would start with Mr Penshurt's enemies.'

'We'll make a detective out of you yet, Richie. Now home please, and remember, if you win the toss ...'

She joined him as they spoke together. '... you always bat first!'

Dr Jock McAdam was right when he told detectives they might have more luck with forensics. There were smudged prints on the cardboard sign with the words *Tommy Bent*. There were footprints in the sand around where the body was found. Those footprints, some were flat shoes, others not so flat, were found near the bathing box and then walking to the spot in the undergrowth where poor old Harry was found. There was a partial fingerprint on the belt designed to keep Harry's trousers from heading south. And there were fibre fragments on Harry's clothing. All the police needed now was a hit on who owned or created such evidence.

The technical gurus went to town on Harry's financial affairs. Most accounts had withdrawals for just under the maximum amount allowed. Withdrawing before midnight, and then after, close to the witching hour, on some accounts gave the crims two bites of the cherry.

Freezing his accounts was essential but an intense search turned up multiple uses of his credit card, gold of course, being used before and after midnight on the day he died.

Use of the card never happened at ATMs or other public places where cameras operated 24/7. The person or persons helping themself to Harry's cash or using the card to send cash overseas, knew what they were doing.

Chapter 38
Everyone's invited

Christine suggested it and Patricia loved the idea. The two new extended families should have a get-together, celebrate the sisters' new found relatives, blood relations or not. Jean hesitated but finally agreed.

'Where will we meet?' she asked Patricia.

'Christine offered her place. They have a really big back yard and provided the weather's fine, people can spread out,' said big sister. 'We set the date and each of us contact our family members and invite them.'

And that's what they did. The weather gods smiled. Paul fired up the barbie, people arrived in dribs and drabs with the sisters out front greeting every arrival and introducing them to the "other family." What an afternoon.

Patricia was chatting to James Friend telling him how much her sister appreciated him spotting her, and helping bring Jean and her son, Graeme back together.

She heard something which didn't sound friendly, looked towards a corner of the garden, and saw her granddaughter, Vicky and her boyfriend, Gavin, having a bit of an argument. Their voices weren't raised but Vicky's body language was enough for Grandma to realize something was wrong. She wanted to intervene but didn't.

Her thoughts were, it may not be serious and besides, who would make a scene on such a happy occasion. She stored the incident in her memory bank and the subject changed when James raised a new topic.

'Graeme told me about the chap found dead on Brighton Beach. He said you and Jean were all members of the same Probus club.'

'We are and the man killed was our president.'

'Goodness. And do the police reckon he was murdered?'

'They do. Of course Jean and I are following the case.'

'Really? Are you the Misses Marple of Brighton?' He smiled but Patricia bit her tongue. 'Have you thought about setting a trap for the killer?'

Patricia froze. All the fun and games happening around her, the people splashing in the pool, the laughter, the talking, eating and drinking all went silent as she pondered the question.

'I'm not sure I follow,' she said.

'Well who better than fellow members of a Probus club to help solve the mystery? Step forward the Probus sisters.' He indicted her with an open hand. Patricia looked shocked. James was serious. 'There are all sorts of ways Agatha Christie helped expose the murderer in her novels.'

Patricia could not have paid more attention. 'Can you give me an example?'

'You mean you've not read Agatha Christie or watched her films?'

'No I have, many times, but not from the point of view of studying her plots.'

'I read somewhere that sometimes she wouldn't decide on the killer until she reached the penultimate chapter.'

'Is that true?' asked Patricia showing her skeptical side.

'I've no idea but if the police struggle to solve the case, perhaps you and Graeme's Mum could do a spot of sleuthing yourselves.'

He smiled and Patricia was busting to explain PUDA. She didn't but made a mental note to take the advice of her new friend, James Friend.

The day was a hit. Not only were the sisters now connected to those in their extended families, some members of said families discovered one another. Jean's son Graeme and Patricia's son-in-law Paul belonged to the same golf club, and Patricia's grandson's wife and Graeme's adopted daughter both did their undergraduate nursing training at Swinburne University.

Farewells were fond and future connections looked promising. With people leaving, the two Probus ladies were helping with the tidy-up.

Patricia spotted Vicky resisting Gavin's request to leave together. She wanted to stay and help her mother. He stormed off.

Patricia found herself alone with her daughter and decided to bite the bullet.

'Christine, there's something I would like to tell you.'

'Oh Mum, you haven't given birth to another daughter?' Her eyes sparkled but lost their happiness when she saw her mother's face. 'What's wrong?'

Patricia struggled. 'It's probably not my place and please tell me to mind my own business but I'm worried about Vicky and her boyfriend.'

Christine became serious. 'You're not interfering. She's your flesh and blood as much as mine. So what's troubling you?'

'He disrespects her. I would never interfere because it's not my place to do so but I just wanted to share my concern with you. I'm sorry.'

Christine kissed her mother. 'I thought we agreed you are never to apologize ever again.'

Patricia forced a smile and Jean arrived. It was time for the sisters to leave. What a day. In the car, they talked non-stop about the get-together. Both were still coming to terms with the fact their lives had been turned upside down.

'A few weeks ago,' said Jean, 'we were two elderly women with only ourselves, my estranged son, and our friends at Probus for company. Now we've got family members coming out of our ears. Isn't it fantastic?'

Patricia showed less enthusiasm.

'Patricia?' asked her sister. 'Why, all of a sudden, are you quiet?'

'I may have done the wrong thing.'

'Oh no! What's happened?'

Patricia explained her worry about Vicky and her boyfriend and how she raised the matter with Christine.

'Me and my big mouth. I was hopeless as a mother and now I'm hopeless as a grandmother.'

So distressed, she pulled over and started to cry. Jean was in shock. After all the changes, the wonderful changes to both their lives, now a simple concern for a family member has caused their world to crash.

Jean tried her best to help her sister, and argued, gently, and reckoned it was no big deal. 'You never know, you may have saved Vicky from a nasty relationship. Come on, my dear, remember what our mother used to say.'

Patricia stopped crying. That was a strange comment from her sister. Their mother was long gone and although talked about from time to time, what Jean said made Patricia stop crying. She genuinely didn't know what her sister meant.

'What did Mother say?'

'You know, time heals all wounds.' Then Patricia remembered and joined her sister in finishing their mother's quote courtesy of Robert Bloch.

'And time wounds all heels.'

Patricia managed a smile. 'Thank you, sister. I hope I haven't done any lasting damage.'

'You haven't done any damage because your heart's in the right place.'

They looked at one another and both felt better.

'Come on,' said Jean, 'I need to get home and water my back garden.'

Patricia drove off and hadn't been going far when she shocked her sister a second time.

'I had a lovely chat with your son's partner.'

'I thought we agreed we would refer to James as Graeme's husband, or as my son-in-law.'

Wow, thought Patricia. *My sister really has grabbed with both hands this second chance at being a mother.*

'As I was saying,' continued Patricia, 'your son-in-law thought we were both Miss Marple and should investigate Harry's murder.'

Jean came alive and turned angry. 'Oh Patricia, you didn't tell him about PUDA!'

'Of course not. But he made a useful suggestion.' Jean stared at the driver. 'Tell me,' said Patricia, 'what do you know about Agatha Christie?'

Chapter 39
Bingo!

The cops got a hit. Forensics sent across reports of DNA samples found at the beachside crime scene. The results were run through the data bases and bingo, somebody was identified. Richie delivered the good news to her boss.

'He's a what?' asked Righteous looking at the screed showing the face and details of the suspect.

'Apparently he's a car thief, minor drug dealer and cross-dresser.'

'And his DNA was found on the body of Harry Penshurst?'

'Not the body but on the belt of the victim, the one which failed to keep Harry's strides from ending up around his ankles.'

Righteous scratched his chin. 'Is this a minor breakthrough or the straw that breaks the camel's back?' He looked at Richie and grinned. 'Let's have the gentleman in drag pay us a visit.'

'Sir,' said the detective sergeant and left.

Two hours before the DNA discovery, Terry, brother-in-law of the victim, was half asleep in his unmade bed with its unwashed sheets and thinking about what he'd do with his share of Harry's dough. If his sister scored the lot, surely she'd get squillions, so how much would Terence pocket and what would he spend it on. Ah, day dreaming. It's true. Sometimes just thinking about the journey is better than the actual event itself.

But amidst his happy thoughts was one seriously unhappy one. Then it came to life. A loud door knock sounded particularly police-like.

Terry thought about lying low hoping they'd go away. Then he pictured cops yelling, giving a warning before whipping out the big red key, and changing from knocking to smashing. His front door could be pushed in with a feather duster.

'All right!' he yelled slash grumbled, and fell out of bed. He built up a face of hatred to confront the grinning pigs. He opened the door and the visitors were sure grinning.

But they were not from Victoria Police being none other than those minor-league crims, Peter, Paul, and Mary. Strangely, on this occasion, Mary was Patrick sans wig or even a spot of lippy. He looked like the ugly bloke he was.

The trio didn't wait for an invitation but were in before Terry could say, 'Good morning and won't you step inside?' Mary, the official family bouncer, waited at the door preventing Terry from doing a runner. For Terry that would be a limper.

He joined the brothers in his kitchen now officially a bomb site.

'Guys, g'day, how are we?' said Terry with enough bonhomie to fill a mosquito's suitcase.

'We is here, Terence, me old mate, to discuss cash,' said Peter who needed massive funds to pay for the work required on his teeth.

'Readies,' said Paul who grinned inspiring the song, *All I Want for Christmas is my Two Front Teeth.*

'Big readies,' added Patrick who looked more attractive as a man and that wasn't saying much.

Terry knew this would happen. The boys had given him part of Willim without an *a* to bury in a certain Brighton backyard—they could say backyard now because Henry wasn't around to scream "rear garden." And for said body part, Terry would pay the brothers a tasty consideration.

'Look lads, you know I'm good for that body part. My sister is due big dough any day now. She gets paid, I get paid and you get paid. Okay?'

Not okay.

'Keep y'money,' said Peter, and Terry thought he would die of shock. He spluttered. 'Sorry?'

'We can give you that chopped specimen for nix. That was a taster, a freebie to thank you for your next big order.'

'Oh,' squeaked Terry. 'What next big order?'

The brothers became Cheshire cats. Their laughter became infectious. Nice joke, Tel. They mocked him. 'What next big order?

'You know, that whole body order. Your bruvva-in-law. And for him we definitely do want our share.'

'Definitely,' babbled the other brothers.

'Now we need to agree a figure,' sneered Peter.

'A figure,' echoed Paul.

'A very big figure,' from Patrick whose stubble even threatened.

'Right,' said Terry now wanting to raise his hand and be excused. What the hell was going on?

'We knocked him,' said Peter raising his voice. 'That big ticket item, your sister's old man, that bloke with the overweight super fund, we put him away just like you requested.'

Terry said something and it wasn't, 'Damn good job, chaps. You are simply the best.'

'So once we agree the price, Terence,' said Peter, 'all we need right now is the date on which them funds will be delivered. Comprendi?'

'Yes, yes. I mean Si, si,' said a panic-struck brother-in-law. Never more did he wish to have the cops turn up on his doorstep. He'd told the brothers about his sister wanting her prick of a husband to disappear and now he had. Now the boys had fulfilled their part of the bargain and he needed to pay up or suffer. He tried not to imagine the torture the lads would inflict on his body, the only one he had, if he withheld the coin.

'Wanna know how we done it?' grinned Paul.

That was a wrong comment and big brother Peter whacked him. 'I told you not to tell nobody.'

'Sorry, sorry,' quivered mouse-like Paul.

Terry was desperate to delay. 'No really, guys, I'm interested. My sister will love to hear how he snuffed it. Please, go ahead.'

Peter wheezed. 'All right and I've gotta admit we had a bit of luck.'

Patrick piped up. 'We had a *lotta* luck.'

'Any chance of a brew?' asked Peter which was more of an order and Terry moved with speed to make coffee. Finding four mugs was tricky. Finding four clean ones, impossible.

'We was out on the bay to pick up a bundle of coke dropped overboard from this cargo ship,' said Peter with his brothers grinning.

'Wow, big time,' said Terry trying to ingratiate himself into the gang.

'Disaster,' said Peter. 'We broke down, couldn't find the package, which is another reason why we need your dough asap, and were floating in choppy seas, as you might say, up Shit Creek without a paddle.'

143

'But we did have a paddle, two,' said Paul. The look he got from big brother saw him cower into silence. Peter continued.

'We was drifting and finally got closer to land. We set off from around Dromana and, would you believe, we came ashore in Brighton.'

Terry was never more attentive. 'Brighton? Wow!'

'There was all these little sheds painted in whacky colours.'

'Bathing boxes,' offered Terry now starting a minor tremble.

'So we drag the boat up on the sand and start looking for a car to nick to get home. We're stomping through the sand and then we strike gold. We get to this bathing box and there's a bloke propped up against it. We move in, shine a torch on his smiling face, and Mary recognizes him.'

'It was that bloke, the one you asked us to knock. We couldn't believe our luck,' said Mary boasting of his facial recognition skills. 'The guy was asleep, probably pissed. I mean how easy was it to do the business. We carried the body into the undergrowth, dropped his daks, and scarpered.'

Peter delivered the epilogue. 'We nicked a motor, got home, grabbed some tools, come back, fixed the boat and sailed off into the sunset.'

'Sunrise,' added Mary.

'What?' snapped his brother.

'Sun*rise*. It was morning not night. We sailed off into the sun*rise*.'

Peter had a look reminiscent of the Cain and Abel tale, with the older brother playing the older brother Cain. Mary dropped the subject.

'Bloody marvellous,' said Terry now even more desperate to raise his hand and ask to be excused. He got brave. 'You didn't mention how you finished him off.'

'Oh that was another stroke of luck,' said Peter. 'We was carrying him from the beach to the bushes, gotta hide the stiff, and Mary stumbled. She accidentally sat on his chest. The fat bastard gave out this wheeze and carked it. Job done.'

'Brilliant,' said Terry wanting to scream in fear and disbelief.

'So we'll leave it with you, Tel,' said Peter. 'As much as we love making house calls and drinking your revolting coffee,' he spat, 'please don't make us come back. You come to us, mate, with a nice big brown paper bag full of used notes, the dough we lost on that box of coke sunk in the bay.'

He slapped Terry. 'Come on lads, farting is such sweet sorrow and all that jazz.' Peter led his laughing brothers out of Terry's tip.

The tenant closed his paper thin front door then sprinted to the loo.

'Shit!' he screamed, which was appropriate.

Chapter 40
Oops!

Richie, in the company of two detective constables, arrived at the Murphy des res. The lads were not long home from giving Terry the terrifying news about the late Henry Penshurst, and politely requesting payment for services rendered. Terry got the partial arm for nix but the complete body of Harry was worth a motza. Terry was desperate to tell Big Sis, beg for an early downpayment, and the Murphy brothers were hoping to see the cash yesterday.

Paul opened the door and swore.

'Good day, Mr Murphy. Is your brother Patrick in?' asked Richie.

'Nuh.' This was an automatic response. Forget AI, the Murphy brothers were programmed from birth to reply with silence, "nuh," or a "No comment."

'Well you won't mind if we come in and wait.'

Richie stepped forward and Paul tried to become Michelin Man and fully fill the space of the doorway. No chance.

The boss arrived. 'What's goin' on?' asked Peter barging through to repel boarders.

'Police, Mr Murphy,' said Richie displaying her badge. 'We're here to arrest your brother, Patrick.'

'What for?' demanded the boss of the gang.

'Your other brother here said he was not in.'

Paul got smart. Doomed from the start. 'Oh, you mean my sister, Mary.'

Peter snapped at Richie, furious that any cop would knock on his door, let alone a woman. 'Where's your warrant?'

Richie repelled bullshit with ease. 'Where's Patrick Murphy?'

Before fisticuffs and additional threats evolved, Patrick pushed forward. 'I'm here.' He wore a fetching outfit of grubby jeans, grubby shirt, untied boots designed to crush beer bottles and cans, and no wig. His hair, footwear and clothing may have contained DNA from any number of crimes.

The constables moved forward drawing the arrestee from the house and gifting him a free pair of silver bracelets.

'Patrick Murphy,' said the DS, 'I'm arresting you on suspicion of murder.'

The arrested brother exploded. His siblings hissed and snarled.

'You have the right to remain silent and ...' recited Richie although no-one heard the rest of her speech with all three brothers speaking and screaming their protests. As he was being led away, Peter yelled.

'Zip it, Mary.'

Paul backed his brother. 'Yeah, and don't say nothing either!'

Bobby the bobby was making Glenda a drink when their front door bell sounded. He was surprised to see fellow Probus member Lionel Carruthers.

'Hello Lionel. How are you?'

'Good morning Bob. Sorry to show up unannounced but I wonder if you can spare a few minutes.'

'Of course, come in, come in.'

Bobby needed to make decisions on various occasions when his wife was in the vicinity. Sometimes he kept people away from her when he thought she should or need not be involved. This was one such occasion.

'Come this way, Lionel,' he said and placed the visitor in the study. I won't be a minute.' He ducked back to the kitchen, poured Glenda her drink and explained to her how he had some Probus business to address. When he returned, Lionel was profuse in his apologies. Bobby put him at ease.

'Lionel, please, you have not disturbed anyone. Now sit, my friend, and tell me your news.' The visitor became doubly serious. 'I hope you haven't come to tell me my Probus subs are overdue.'

Bobby offered a weak grin. Lionel tried to copy him but failed.

Silence. Lionel didn't know where to start and Bobby gave him a prompt. 'I hope it's not bad news.'

'It's about our former president.' That cleared the decks. 'First I should tell you my opinion of Harry changed dramatically just before he died. Bobby noted his visitor didn't say, 'was killed'.'

Lionel related the whole story about Harry's scheme to obtain an award, and how he deceived Lionel and several others. Bobby pondered this news. It didn't seem far-fetched, in fact highly believable.

'I'm deeply sorry to hear that, Lionel. I know we shouldn't speak ill of the dead but this could be an exception. But I'm curious as to why you would tell me this story and now.' He corrected himself. 'This *true* story.'

Lionel took a deep breath and the pictures on the walls in Bobby's office craned their frames to hear.

'I think my wife might have killed Harry Penshurst.'

Patricia couldn't shake her feelings of guilt having told Christine she disapproved of Vicky's boyfriend. The grandmother had been on the scene for three minutes and here she was, running the family telling them who was allowed in and who not as if she'd been in charge for half a century. *Mind your own business, Patricia.*

Jean tried to stop her sister from worrying but the guilt hung around like an unpleasant smell.

Keep busy was Patricia's motto and she dusted where she dusted two hours ago. Saved by the bell as someone arrived at her front door.

It was déjà vu only without the rain. A dry granddaughter stood there looking sad and depressed.

'Oh Gran, can I come in please?'

Vicky began to cry and was led inside. The women hugged. In the lounge, they sat where they first met. Patricia played it well allowing the young woman to settle and recover before asking a single question.

'Now, young lady, my favourite granddaughter, what on Earth is troubling you? And should we have some tea because I know you're a tea girl.'

Vicky loved this elderly lady she'd only just met and felt at ease unburdening her heart. She spoke but tears accompanied her speech.

'Oh Gran, Gavin's cheating on me.'

Patricia handed her a box of tissues and even tugged at the one poking out of the box. Vicky wiped her eyes and blew her nose as her grandmother listened, shared her pain but sensed a snippet of satisfaction that her assessment of the boyfriend appeared to be spot on.

'I was in The Glen shopping centre and there he was in the corner of the coffee shop kissing a girl. They were serious and I felt sick.'

Patricia squeezed her hand. 'Well I didn't give your Mum any advice on boys as I was only her mother for a few days but here's my two bob's worth.'

Vicky looked puzzled. 'I don't know what two bob's worth means.'

Patricia grinned and her smile made Vicky smile. 'Two bob is twenty cents. I mean my advice may not be worth much but I'm happy to help if I can.'

'I'm sure with all your wisdom, your advice will be brilliant.'

Patricia took a deep breath. 'Okay, here goes. One, you are lucky to escape Mr Two-Timer before you got stuck with him and two, there are plenty more fish in the sea. And besides, any granddaughter of mine deserves the very best in suitors. In fact send any prospects around, and I'll vet them.'

They hugged, laughed, had a cuppa and chatted for an enjoyable time where the two women cemented their love and affection for one another. Patricia insisted on driving Vicky home. There, they were welcomed by the middle member of the three generations of females. When Vicky told her mother the story, the two older women exchanged a glance with Christine winking at her mother.

Nice one, Mum. Nice one, Gran.

Chapter 41
Well done Agatha

Patrick or Mary or both were in trouble. He'd been in a cop shop before and the drill was simple. Say nothing, lawyer up and learn your lines till you can recite them in your sleep. Two words do not a big speech make.

'No comment,' was delivered in a monotone with no emphasis, tempi variation or accent. The police gave him more rope with which to hang himself keeping their powder dry. The Murphy cross-dresser grew more confident. Asking him for his movements on the night in question, he gave them nothing and knew his brothers would have him at home sewing sequins on his latest little black number—actually it was a big little black number he snapped up at a charity shop in Frankston—providing him with an iron-clad alibi.

Richie grew impatient. 'We have your DNA on a belt worn by the victim, the dead body found in the undergrowth at Brighton beach, Mr Murphy. Can you explain how it got there? The DNA I mean, not the dead body, although both would be acceptable?'

The "No comment" took longer to arrive.

'We have a photo of you and two other individuals, I'll bet my pension they're your brothers, on the beach at Brighton on the night you were at home with your sewing kit.' She passed across the table a copy of an A4 picture taken by a hidden sensor-controlled still camera set up on the foreshore to catch vandals, druggies and drunks around the tourist attraction, the bathing boxes. Patrick was downstage centre and looking at the camera. He wasn't grinning but it was an excellent likeness.

'Any comment, Mr Murphy?' He grunted. 'Your dress looks nice.'

Mary snarled and wanted to die. The three brothers missed the cocaine dropped overboard and lost a fortune. They were ripped off anyway—poor quality goods. And, of course, there's no "on tick" terms of trade when dealing with South American drug cartels. At least the Australian Navy don't shoot first and make pathetic excuses later.

Then the brothers' luck changed when their tinnie, with a hat, broke down and they came ashore at Brighton only to stumble upon Terry's wealthy brother-in-law, dozing thanks to the anaesthetic administered by a certain dental nurse. Her assistant, armed with a camera and cardboard sign, stood ready. Harry's killer, well one of them, was snookered.

Bobby struggled to understand Lionel's statement, 'I think my wife might have killed Harry Penshurst.' Lionel was the stereotypical accountant. White shirt, plain tie, bland suit or jacket, short back and sides haircut, and someone who spoke in public on very few occasions. Now he's made what at first hearing sounds like a ridiculous claim.

'Can you give me a little bit more information, Lionel?'

He did, explaining how his distress, thanks to Harry, made his wife seriously angry.

'She only met Harry the once but didn't like him from the off. He acted like an over-aged, overweight Lothario with only one attractive feature, his money.'

Bobby nodded. 'I can't speak for the fairer sex but that does sound pretty accurate. But even if your wife hated Harry, that doesn't mean she murdered him. Are you sure you're not reading too much into this?'

Lionel had clearly given the matter a lot of thought. 'Here's what happened. It started with Naomi taking phone calls at odd hours. When I asked, she brushed it off as someone from work.'

'What does your wife do?'

'Dental nurse. She's worked at the same clinic for decades and the place wouldn't be nearly as efficient without her.'

'Right,' said Bobby still unsure where this was going.

'The other day I emptied the kitchen bin and wrapped inside a plastic bag was something I didn't recognize.'

Bobby never examined the contents of his kitchen bin. He tied the inside bag in two knots, lifted it and dropped it in the outside bin. Obviously, Lionel was fussy. He needed to get out more.

'I unwrapped the small plastic bag and found a medical container, empty but with the label intact. It read *Anaesthetic*. It's the sort of thing she would have handled a thousand times.'

'Anaesthetic? To put a patient to sleep?'

'Yes, and why would she have brought that home?'

'Did you ask her about it?'

'Lord no, I was too scared. You've got to help me, Bob. Do I go to the police and report her? I've lost my faith in humankind thanks to Penshurst. I don't want to lose my wife because his cruelty drove her to kill him.'

Bobby struggled. If true, this was more than serious. If not, he needed to bring Lionel down from his distressed state.

'You may be completely wrong, Lionel. You may have jumped to the wrong conclusion. And taking the devil's advocate position, how do you murder someone with anaesthetic? All a local does is make one side of your face go numb for half an hour, at least that's my experience.'

'So you think I'm mistaken? You're a police officer.'

'Retired.'

'But do you think it's suspicious?'

Bobby made a face and raised his hands. 'How do we take anaesthetic? By injection. Is your wife trained in giving injections? And even if she is, how does Harry co-operate? Can you see Harry agreeing to having a needle stuck in him from someone he barely knows on Brighton beach at midnight?'

Lionel drew breath. This was the first time he didn't answer.

'And was she out on the night Harry was murdered?' Lionel was a heavy sleeper. 'Look my friend,' said Bobby. 'Let me think about it and I'll get back to you with my thoughts and suggestions.'

'When?'

It was Bobby's turn to draw breath. 'End of the week?'

Lionel wasn't happy but agreed. Bobby showed him out and Glenda asked about the visitor.

The retired police officer did a Naomi and brushed off his wife's enquiry. 'Just someone from work, my dear.'

'You're retired,' she drawled.

'Not from Probus, I'm not.'

Chapter 42
The panic begins

Terry panicked and cursed his big mouth. Why, oh why did he invite the Murphy brothers to bump off his brother-in-law? He did know why. His sister more or less ordered him to, and if he did, big bucks would flow.

And look at his previous dealings with the boys. The trio provided him a chopped limb from their earlier homicide which Terry used to embarrass the current victim. Sadly, the embarrassment didn't lead to a heart attack.

And now, oh my godfather, now how unlucky can one be? The brothers break down out on the Bay, drift, land ashore a hundred metres from where the stupefied Harry sits, snoring, waiting to be murdered. Their outrageous luck puts Terry in the proverbial.

He had to report to his sister, must tell her before she finds out. If she found out from another source, baby brother was a dead man stumbling. Of course, once he delivered said report, he'd become eligible to sing in the Vienna Boys' Choir.

'Yes?' came Margaret's voice over the intercom.

'It's me,' said Terry automatically trying to disguise his voice.

The gate opening sound began and the siblings met.

'I don't want to hear anything, anything other than good news that involves me getting easy access to Harry's money and you being a million miles from whoever killed him.

Terry hesitated and Margaret knew things were bad.

Once he started explaining what happened with the Murphy brothers, she fell silent and when Terry's tale ended, she was so enraged she couldn't speak. The salt in the wound was the luck, good, bad or in-between, he wasn't sure, the trio had in landing ashore where they did.

'That's the sad and sorry tale, Sis. At least we ain't involved in his death and once those idiots are charged and sent down, the funds from the bastard's accounts should start to flow.'

Her pain was exquisite. His almost as bad, no, worse.

'Those brothers are good at torture, murder and hacking bodies,' he said. 'If you can't pay me, I'm dead.'

'Good,' she said.

He screamed. 'Good? I did exactly what you asked, no, ordered me to do. I kept my part of the bargain. Now you must keep your part.'

'And if I don't? What then?'

Tricky question for poor old Terry. What would he gain by attacking his sister, or being a grass, anathema to his very being? He could pinch Harry's watches, cufflinks, and ancient bottles of Scotch. Big deal. But a dead or incarcerated sibling would achieve nothing.

Bobby sent word to Patricia and Jean. Both saw the text, responded immediately and Patricia rang her sister.

'I'll pick you up in ten minutes,' said Big Sister.

'This must be super important,' said Jean. 'Why meet asap?'

'Yes, well the sooner we stop gasbagging and get ready, the sooner we'll find out. Go!' Jean copped a dial tone and did as ordered.

In the car on the short drive to Bobby and Glenda's home, they exhausted every possibility. Bobby took them into the back garden where Glenda sat in the shade. The sisters wanted the meeting to start but Bobby wanted his wife to enjoy some solid social contact. He'd read an article online—how much of what appears online is true or even remotely so?—which stated that a lack of social contact helps age the brain. He wanted his wheelchair-bound wife to keep her brain as healthy as possible for as long as possible. Chat with the sisters was so ordered.

Socializing over, the members of PUDA sat in his study where Bobby hesitated. The sisters reckoned they were in for some shocking news.

'I'm struggling, ladies, because my news was told to me in confidence. Let me tell you what I've heard from the police. They have a man in custody, someone with a police record, who has been charged with Harry's murder.'

'Do we know him?' asked Jean bordering on breathless.

Bobby shook his head. 'The police are sure he didn't act alone but as yet, only one man has been arrested.' He paused. 'The other news is tricky. It didn't come from the police but from one of our own.'

'Someone from Probus?' gasped Patricia, and Bobby nodded.

'This person believes their spouse killed Harry.'

Organ stops, from an old-fashioned organ where the player pedals to create the wind to make the sound, and pulls out the stops to change the sound, are words used to describe shock. It applied in this situation. The sisters displayed their reaction when their eyes became like organ stops. Both were busting for names, well, one name.

'I hope you can appreciate the sensitivity of the situation,' continued Bobby. 'If the claim is true, we must tell the police. If it's not, and we speak about it outside this room, we could do serious harm to the individuals involved. We could even destroy a marriage.'

'So what will we do?' asked Jean now worried, excited, and confused. This to her was a form of multi-tasking.

'Well I'd like to hear your thoughts, ladies. PUDA is an equal opportunity organization. All for one and one for all or something like that. Speak up, please.'

The sisters looked at one another and Patricia gave a tiny nod.

'I'm happy to be guided by you, sir,' said Jean. 'You're the experienced police officer.'

Bobby smiled at Jean then looked at Patricia.

'I've been thinking about how to catch Harry's killer, and Jean's son-in-law suggested Agatha Christie.' The others paid rapt attention and Jean pedalled harder on her old-fashioned organ.

'Agatha Christie? How do you mean?' asked Bobby.

'Two things come to mind. She once used multiple murderers and already Harry's death may fit that model. The police have arrested Person A and one of our own Probus members has told you their spouse, Person B, is also a possible killer. Agatha Christie had a case where there were multiple murderers. Perhaps we should investigate Person B, and if we reckon he or she is involved, then we can tell the police.'

'I like that idea,' said Jean.

'Yes, okay Patricia, but you said two things come to mind.'

'It's something else Agatha Christie did and involves anonymous letters. We send a letter to someone we think knows something about Harry's killer and watch their reaction.'

'Goodness,' said Jean shocked at both the suggestion and the thinking going on inside her sister's head.

'Can you give us an example?' asked Bobby.

'We send an anonymous, old-fashioned snail mail with the words, "I know who killed Harry." That's all, nothing else.'

'But if you change the word *I* to *We,* it will increase the pressure, meaning there are others who think the same,' suggested Bobby.

'Agreed,' said Patricia.

'Yes but who gets the letter?' asked Jean trying to catch up.

Patricia paused then spoke with conviction. 'Margaret Penshurst.'

Chapter 43

The grass in the snake

The Get Harry kidnap went well. Carter and Naomi kept the kick off details from their co-conspirators until the last minute. The male attackers, with one dry run already under their belt, surprised Harry, got him away and their threats terrified the Probus president who gave up his banking details under fear of serious pain or death. Thank you, Harry.

The victim was driven to the beach at Brighton and held down while the female attackers gave him an injection of anaesthetic. The boys disappeared. Harry was posed against a bathing hut, decorated with a *Tommy Bent* sign and had his photo taken. Several times. Leaving him to sleep it off, the females fled. Harry was alive but his life was ruined.

Enter the killers direct from the waters of Port Phillip Bay.

Of course every super fund has severe restrictions on the removal of money. Half a mill on two clicks of a mouse. I don't think so.

But the two kidnappers got a nice little earner and used Harry's credit cards for a top up. The silly bugger even had over 300 bucks in his wallet and naturally, that disappeared as well.

Spiteri was a ladies' man. His European heritage provided the looks, and his charm around women worked more often than not. At the time he began planning to attack Penshurst with the other victim who planted carrots in his back garden, Spiteri was courting a woman. Valerie was single (at the time), attractive, not short of a bob and who ran an employment agency, a front for an escort agency. What she saw in Spiteri was anyone's guess. Twice divorced Valerie enjoyed the company of men who splashed the cash. Joseph at first took Valerie to quality restaurants. Nice but not in the premier league. Approaching the kidnap and robbery of the Probus president and the expected influx of funds, Joseph changed gear.

He took his favourite businesswoman slash madam out to top of the town establishments. He liked showing off.

Their relationship simmered rather than boiled but she appreciated the more upmarket lifestyle and took the commitment to the next level. All that euphemism talk in reality meant they took to regular bouts of horizontal dancing. More euphemisms.

Joe loved his new life. He fancied his woman, she was loaded and he could help in her business plans, meaning his life was a bit of all right. The only fly in the ointment was the booze. He liked to drink. A lot.

Alas, as was the case with all of Valerie's former beaus, Joe's value devalued. He was no longer the guy for her. She was good at giving men the flick but Joe was different.

She reckoned he could get nasty. She was right there. He'd never been angry with her but she sensed a vein of entitlement just below the surface and started a slow process of dumping Mr Spiteri.

The PUDA meeting saw the first vote take place. This was serious. Not only minute taking but now motions being put to the board. Of course a second was required and in a body of three, a second could be a struggle.

'Okay,' said the Chair, Bobby[2], 'the question is do we investigate the spouse of the Probus member who came to visit Robert Ayers? Do we have a second?' Both sisters raised a hand. 'In favour please indicate.'

Again the sisters raised a hand in concert.

Bobby raised his. 'Passed unanimously,' he said and Jean added the minute to the minutes. The pressure switched to the Chair.

'Before I announce the member's name, I need to remind both of you ladies that discussion of this and any other PUDA business outside of our meetings is strictly forbidden. Agreed?'

Both women said, 'Agreed.'

Patricia had a question. 'What's the difference between "forbidden" and "strictly forbidden"?'

Jean complained. 'Oh don't, Patricia. Sorry Bobby but she can be like this. It's all her training as a lawyer's clerk.'

'Thank you, Jean, and I was a paralegal.'

Bobby, as Chair, doubled as referee. 'Let's not fall out ladies but understand that if we reveal which cardinal we voted for, we are being unfair to the new pope.'

The women had no idea where that came from but got the message. Zip it.

'The Probus member who came to see me was Lionel Carruthers.' Bobby told the background story which shocked the sisters.

'That's a horrible thing to do,' said Jean. 'Harry was a cruel man.'

Patricia agreed but pushed for action. 'So how do we manage the accusation?'

'I was thinking one or both of you ladies could interview Lionel's wife. Her name is Naomi. The feminine approach might be better and especially as I'm ex-police.'

'But how do we approach her without betraying Lionel?' asked Patricia.

Bobby paused for thought. 'How about you tell the truth? You've heard stories about Harry making promises he never kept and see if she bites. You care about Lionel. What we need to do is prove Lionel is wrong about his wife. You need to follow her and get her alone.'

'And what if she confesses to murder?'

Bobby pondered. 'Let's cross that bridge when we get to it.'

Valerie wanted rid of Joseph Spiteri. Out of fear, she held back. Then came a lucky break. With alcohol overlap, one night Joe started boasting more than usual.

'You know, babe, I told you how some scumbag ripped me off in a real estate deal?'

'Yes,' replied Valerie plying her current lover with another glass.

'Well I fixed the prick and "borrowed" some of his ill-gotten gains.'

He laughed enjoying the memory of kidnapping Harry Penshurst and accessing his bank accounts before passing him along the chain to a couple of women who had their own beef with the man.

Valerie got nosy asking questions that teased Spiteri. He thought she was interested in him, in his prowess to commit serious crime and get away with it. He told all and Valerie discovered gold. She couldn't throw out pisspot Spiteri but someone else could.

158

The next day, when alone, she rang the police and ended up speaking to Detective Sergeant Grace Benaud, aka Richie who was keen to chat with this new potential witness, aka a grass.

The sisters buzzed. Not only were they founding members of PUDA, they were handed their first assignment. Investigate the wife of a Probus member and discover if she murdered their late president. Goodness, this is serious.

Ideas were tossed around. They knew Lionel's address and his wife worked for a dental surgery. Next morning they set off early. Patricia drove and Jean took notes. They parked near the Carruthers' house. Schoolkids walked past and those who looked into the parked vehicle quickly lost interest when the occupants were two old biddies examining what looked like a map. Anyway, almost all the kids were on their phone.

Naomi drove into the street and headed away from them. They followed with Jean playing traffic cop or bad cop or confused septuagenarian.

'Don't get too close,' she said more than once.

'Jean! I know what I'm doing.'

Naomi turned into a quiet street in Moorabbin (another of Tommy Bent's stamping grounds) and stopped. Patricia did likewise. Naomi hopped out, didn't lock her car, and carrying a large envelope, hurried into a garden designed by a vampire disguised as a ringmaster.

'What's she doing?' asked Jean, and Patricia decided on all future PUDA jobs, she would work alone.

'I don't know. Just wait!' she tried to say without yelling.

Two minutes later Naomi came out, hopped back in her car, and left.

'Follow her,' ordered Jean whose belief in her superiority went to her head.

Patricia drove. 'And get the number of that house including a photo.'

Jean panicked. In trying to grab her phone and take a picture, their car went past and she missed it.

'Ah!' she screamed.

'The number is 27,' said her older sister and the chase continued.

'I'm not stepping inside a police station,' said Valerie.

'Okay,' replied Richie. 'I'm in St Kilda Road near the river. Where would you like to meet?'

'The gardens with the floral clock. Do you know it?'

'Know it? I set my watch by it. How about in an hour?'

'Make it thirty minutes.'

'How will I know you?' asked the detective.

'All black, gold jewellery, blonde beehive.

'And I can call you Val.'

'Yes.' The line went dead.

Starsky and Hutch or rather Abbott and Costello managed to follow Naomi through the streets to what they presumed was her workplace. As the street front signage thundered *Dental Surgery*, they were right. Naomi drove into a covered carpark and Patricia chose not to follow.

'What now?' asked Jean. 'Do we go to reception, make an appointment and hope Naomi is the nurse on duty?'

'If you were a professional detective, that decision would cost you your job. Let's go back to 27 Ronan Road, knock on the door, and see what the occupant has to say.'

'I was going to suggest that,' said Jean.

Patricia made no comment and they found the address.

Standing outside the door, Patricia said, 'I'll do the talking.' It wasn't a request or suggestion but an order.

Nixie Black opened the door holding the only copy, printed at Officeworks, of her magical tome, *Tommy Bent Today* with the cover on display.

She relaxed. These old ladies posed no threat.

'Good morning, ladies, what can I do for you?' said Nixie.

'Good morning,' said Patricia. 'We're sisters interested in local history and are canvassing the area ...'

Patricia's opening patter collapsed as the homeowner recognized Jean.

'Mrs Gilchrist,' she exclaimed and the younger sister came alive.

'Hello,' she said and couldn't remember the woman's name.

'Nixie Black, author, and self-publisher. We met at the library.'

Patricia was forgotten.

'That's right,' said Jean as Nixie's book was thrust forward.

'And here's my finished book.'

'Oh, congratulations.'

The door was pushed open, Nixie's smile was pushed open and her welcome could not have been more genuine.

'Ladies, please do come in.'

Fashion wise, Valerie stood out like a sore thumb. Richie in her small boots, grey tailored slacks, white shirt, and grey jacket would have been a natural in Val's business.

'Hi Val, I'm Richie.' The detective offered her hand and Val's gloved mitt responded.

'Richie? What sort of a name is that?'

'Are you a cricket junkie?' Val's face answered. 'Let's walk.'

Richie set off but stopped because Val stood still.

'Are you recording this?' she asked.

Richie opened her jacket allowing Val to check and admire her slim figure. 'Nothing.' Val caught up and off they went. 'So, what do you know?'

'A boyfriend got drunk and boasted about how he and a mate kidnapped and robbed this bloke. I thought the boyfriend was all mouth and trousers until he mentioned the name—Harry Penshurst.' Richie was rapt. 'I told him he was lying which upset him so he explained how this Harry guy had ripped off him and his chum, Carter Thomas, in development investments, and to get back at Penshurst they persuaded, read threatened and tortured the guy, until he handed over the so-called lost money. Once they got the dough, my ex and his partner handed him over to two women at the bathing boxes on the beach at Brighton. Does that sound interesting?'

Richie smiled. 'It does, Val, and all I need from you is a simple signed statement.'

The grass shrunk. 'Ah no, as I said on the phone, no police station, no statement, no names, no pack drill. But I'll be honest. You will do me one heck of a favour if you arrest the gentleman concerned. I will accept such action as payment in full. Deal?' This time the gloved hand was extended and Richie shook it.

'Deal,' she said and noted the names, Joseph Spiteri and Carter Thomas. Richie knew Carter Thomas, the angler in East Gippsland. But who was Joseph Spiteri and who were the two women and what did they do to the victim?

161

Chapter 44
I smell a denouement

'Great work, Richie,' said Righteous. 'What do we know about this Joseph Spiteri?'

'Sounds a likely lad,' said Benaud. 'We found he was an investor in a development run by the lovely Henry Penshurst where most investors did their dough. I know about guessing but if Spiteri is not an acquaintance or more likely a partner in crime of the boy from Bentleigh with the pebbles in his driveway, I'll go he. Motive is obvious although evidence remains elusive.'

'Right,' said Righteous. 'We need both in here for an interview as soon as. Separate of course. One has a wife, the other a girlfriend. Let's have a chat with the women today, this afternoon.'

'The girlfriend's angry, boss. She wants nothing more than her now ex to go away for a long time.'

Senior Constable Bramble was a thinker. 'But what's the charge? If the girlfriend's testimony is that our lads kidnapped and robbed the victim, hearsay in its purest form, where does murder fit into this case?'

'It doesn't,' said the boss. 'The rest of her tale mentions two women who also had it in for Harry. Who are these women and what did they do?'

'We spotted the Murphy brothers on camera at the beach. Where are the ladies on film and the two robbers?' asked Bramble who, like Richie, was bright and keen on rising within the ranks.

'There are four other bodies caught on camera before the Murphy clan,' said Richie. Two are wearing balaclavas and two are dressed as nuns who could be auditioning for *The Sound of Music*. None can be identified.'

'More homework, folks,' said Righteous, 'and for once, Bramble is right. Where does murder fit into this case? Interviews loomed large.

The sisters sat in Nixie's unusual sitting room. You couldn't call it a lounge because, well you just couldn't. Patricia looked miffed as her role as lead detective had been snatched away.

'So you finally finished your book, Ms Black,' said Jean.

'Call me Nixie, please.' She bubbled. 'Yes, I faced roadblocks but the last one has been removed and it's now non-stop forward to the launch.'

The words "roadblock" and "been removed" were of keen interest to the visitors.

'Oh,' said Patricia wanting back into the team. 'What sort of a roadblock?'

Nixie didn't like the question or the woman asking it. Jean popped back in to restore the friendly atmosphere.

'I remember you were trying to discover some of Tommy Bent's early transactions. How did that go?'

Nixie relaxed. 'Oh, very well thank you. A cousin of mine found one of our relatives was defrauded by Tommy Bent and his partner, and today, a relative of Tommy's partner is alive today and, would you believe, living in Brighton.'

'No,' sounded a shocked Jean.

Patricia was having none of this beating around the bush. 'And would this relative of Tommy Bent's partner happen to be Harry Penshurst?'

Wow, talk about a sudden temperature drop. Nixie started building a brick wall with the expertise of an experienced brickie. Patricia was doing well and kept rolling with the questions.

'We've heard that a wife of a Probus club member here in Brighton hates Harry and wanted to punish him, even murder him.'

'Patricia,' snapped Jean.

'What are you talking about,' threatened Nixie as she piled on another line of bricks.

'We saw Naomi Carruthers deliver an envelope to you only half an hour ago and I wonder what that envelope contained? Incriminating evidence if I'm not mistaken.'

Nixie stood and pointed to the door. 'Get out!' she screamed. 'And never set foot on my property again.' The sisters stood, Jean furious. 'You're lucky I haven't called the police.'

As the sisters left, Patricia got in the last word. '*You're* lucky you didn't call the police. For your sake, let's hope Naomi destroyed the originals.'

In Patricia's car, Jean struggled to speak. 'What have you done?'

'Found out whodunit,' said her sister feeling great inside. She reckoned she could do this sort of thing for a living. Did her new and expansive family know their newly-discovered Grannie was a detective?

Righteous and Richie arrived at Val's town house. She was at work arranging clients for the evening session and as predicted, Spiteri was home. He was searching online for potential business investments. It was close to lunchtime and he answered the door wearing black silk pyjamas.

'Mr Joseph Spiteri,' said DI Righteous showing his badge and giving name and rank with Richie doing the same.

'What do you want?' was tantamount to answering in the affirmative.

'Joseph Spiteri you're under arrest on suspicion of the kidnap and robbery of Henry Penshurst.' Richie moved in with the bracelets.

Spiteri couldn't believe Carter had turned him in, vowed to kill him and, apart from the actual arrest, was mightily miffed to be sprung still wearing pyjamas at lunchtime.

'Can I at least change into some proper clothes?'

The detectives looked at one another, turned their prisoner around and escorted him indoors. He needed the cuffs removed in order to dress and the detectives were not concerned about his modesty. He pretended to be and requested the male leave the room.

'I'm more than happy to undress for you, darling,' he smirked.

Richie looked at his grin and said, 'Two minutes. And you've got nothing I haven't seen already, sir, many, many times before.'

Out in the burbs, two Homicide detectives knocked on the Thomas door. Mrs Thomas answered. 'You're in luck. He only came home this morning.'

Carter wasn't in luck and joined his co-conspirator at Homicide although in separate accommodation. For the police, making arrests is often the easy bit. Turning an arrest into a charge is where it can get tough.

Bobby[2] worked alone. He followed up on the anonymous poisoned pen letter idea thanks to Patricia and her assistant, Agatha Christie. He pushed the intercom outside the Penshurst property.

'Yes?' said Margaret.

'Oh good afternoon, Margaret. It's Robert Ayers from Probus. Have you got a minute?'

There was a pause. Bobby reckoned he could hear her thinking. 'Come in,' she said and the gate unlocked.

He reached the door just as it opened. She went to speak but he got in first and handed her a standard envelope addressed in hand writing to Margaret Penshurst.

'This appears to have been thrown over your fence. I found it on your side of the gate.'

She took it. 'Come in,' she said and led him to the kitchen. 'Coffee?'

'Please.'

He watched as she prepared the coffee and admired the devices atop the granite benchtops. She put the envelope to one side and offered him a choice of coffee. He chose the only one he recognized.

'So, how are you managing?' he asked in his usual friendly manner.

'I'm okay, thanks. I wish the police would release Harry's body. The funeral's been paid for and the grave dug. All we need is his Lordship.'

'Have the police been in touch with how the investigation is going?'

'Nothing.' She brought the coffee to the breakfast table and sat.

'Well as you know, I'm long out of it, but I did hear an arrest has been made. Once the police go public, I'm sure you'll be told.'

'Anything else you've heard?'

'Again don't quote me but I think the person arrested for Harry's murder is the person or is related to the person who buried the human body part in your rear garden.'

Margaret soaked up the information wanting assurance she would never be linked to her late husband's death. Bobby pushed harder.

'Have you had any cranks trying to upset you? Threatening phone calls, anonymous letters, that sort of thing?' She shook her head. He pointed to the envelope he brought with him. 'That envelope tossed over your fence for instance.'

Trapped, she fetched it, sat and opened it. She unfolded the small piece of paper and her face spoke louder than any words. Bobby held out a hand, took the letter, and saw the message.

We know who killed Harry.

Chapter 45
It was a team effort

Some novels have loose ends. Here is a summary, hopefully, a closure of all those found in *Blood Red Roses*.

Nixie Black and Naomi Carruthers

When the female members of PUDA interviewed Nixie, she lost it when Patricia, tired of Jean's softball questions, went hard. Nixie ordered the sisters from her home. Next stop was Naomi. She was the soft target and broke down when confronted by the PUDA detectives. They sat in her car.

'Nixie told us everything,' lied Patricia.

Naomi felt bad. She knew what she did was wrong and couldn't believe their stunt had killed the president.

'We never intended to kill him,' she blurted. 'Those men who Penshurst defrauded agreed to hold him down while Nixie used the hypodermic she borrowed from her father's surgery.'

'What surgery?' asked Patricia.

'Her father's a retired GP. I stole the anaesthetic from work and Nixie had the needle. The two angry men brought the terrified Harry to the beach huts, held him while we put him to sleep.'

'You killed him!' gasped Jean.

'No, not put to sleep as in death, just literally asleep. It made him unconscious or very drowsy. Then we sat him up against the front of a bathing box, hung the *Tommy Bent* sign around his neck, took photos and left him there. He was alive and breathing when we left. All we planned to do was send the photos to the people who award the AO gongs and thus ruin his chances.'

'But now he's dead,' said Patricia. Naomi slumped and wept quietly. 'So if you and Nixie didn't kill him, who did?'

'I don't know,' she sobbed. 'I wish I'd never got involved but when I saw what that horrible man did to Lionel, I had to rescue him. Harry Penshurst never deserved a gong and I'm not sorry he'll never get one.'

The three women sat there listening as Mrs Carruthers cried.

Patricia took charge. 'Naomi, go home to Lionel and say nothing to him or to anyone. Forget the whole thing.'

The shocked dental nurse stared at the elderly women. 'You're letting me go? You're not going to report me to the police?'

'No, we'll say nothing to the police.' said Patricia.

'Lionel has suffered enough,' said Jean. 'You and Nixie didn't kill Harry and we want Lionel to come back to Probus.'

The sisters touched Naomi's shoulder, got out of her car and walked away. She muttered her thanks over and over as her tears continued to fall.

A month after Harry's demise, Nixie launched her *Tommy Bent Today* book. Cousin Michael helped her turn it into an eBook and it was available to download. Nixie knew little about self-publishing and got her first print copies without a barcode. She learnt quickly. A few libraries, a few friends and the Brighton Historical Society all bought a copy. Harry Penshurst kept spinning in his grave.

Carter Thomas and Joseph Spiteri

Getting money out of Penshurst proved to be harder than extracting body fluid from a brick but Harry fancied his own blood. When Spiteri's firearm didn't persuade the fraudster to hand over some of his ill-gotten gains, a pair of secateurs secured around Harry's little right toe, saw the passwords and usernames appear in rapid time.

The key for the kidnappers was to hide the account or accounts into which this new money flowed. Spiteri had the IQ of someone using the password 123456 and a PIN of SPIT.

What a delicious irony when Spiteri's DNA was found in Harry's hair in the form of saliva. Spiteri's spit spat back. His balaclava rode up in the struggle. That, and when Valerie, the former girlfriend and now grass, saying what she did, unrecorded and all hearsay evidence notwithstanding, Joseph decided to raise the white flag. He saved on trial time and expense and hopefully nudged the judge towards less time inside.

Carter was the smart one. Tracing his slice of Penshurst's pile proved tricky. His DNA was never found and there was Buckley's chance he would plead Guilty. His wife couldn't grass him up as he skilfully hid his movements. The prosecution went over the financial losses he made as a result of doing deals with the deceased. The subsequent court case where he lost twice and got financially hammered was mentioned in detail. No-one had a bigger motive to do away with Harry Penshurst than one Carter Thomas.

You can never tell what jury members are thinking. Sometimes the smallest of items, perhaps the weakest piece of evidence can turn a vote from Guilty to Not Guilty or vice versa. In this case, Carter was skittled by a little white pebble. The one recovered from Harry's pocket as he lay in the undergrowth on the beach at Brighton. A white pebble from Carter's driveway. He pleaded Not Guilty, the jury disagreed and for kidnap and robbery, the loser lost again and for these Category 2 offences, he went away for 9 years to serve a minimum of seven. Spiteri got six of the best.

Peter, Paul, and Patrick aka Mary

The brothers Murphy were on a hiding to nothing. Patrick's DNA, his wig hair was found on Harry's hair, and his partial fingerprint was deposited when he pulled down Harry's strides. This evidence stitched up the cross-dresser. And all three were photographed walking ashore after they made landfall when the failed drug run, along with the motor of their tinnie, died on Port Phillip Bay. The Murphy faces were exposed unlike the females before them in their nun outfits and face masks which were returned to the costume hire shop the next day.

The brothers were further cooked by Terry Twomey who turned King's evidence to get out of a charge, any charge, when he made a statement that Patrick Murphy had given him the severed arm of a person unknown, and Terry had buried it thinking the Murphy brothers didn't want any evidence exposed of another murder they recently committed.

Terry was in genuine fear of his life and limb when he buried the body part, or so he said. He lied well. The police reckoned the time and effort to charge him for hiding a body when the body was only 8% whole was not worth the effort, and pot-smoking Tel dodged a bullet. Alas he also dodged a happy ending as is explained in the report on his sibling.

All three brothers were charged with murder and middle sibling, Paul, was seriously unhappy.

'We never killed him,' he protested. 'We was just carrying him. We was making him comfortable when Mary tripped and accidentally landed on him. It wasn't me. And Mary would never have tripped if she hadn't been wearing her stilettos.' Louder. 'I'm not guilty!'

Harry's death was not the first the brothers were involved in. They were lucky Willims without an *a* never got added to the charge sheet. All three will be seriously middle-aged when they next paddle in Port Phillip Bay.

Margaret and Terry

There was a second poison pen letter, this one with the message, *We know what you did last summer* dropped over Margaret's high front fence. Archie found it and used his teeth as a letter-opener. It came to nothing although Margaret's worry beads, she was the most unreligious person in Brighton, got a serious physical and mental workout.

Harry's funeral, manner of death and finances dominated her thinking. The former president's body was finally released and the funeral attracted a bumper crowd. Every member of the Brighton Probus club attended. A number of mourners, more like haters, people who lost money in his schemes came to make sure the bastard was actually dead. When it came to dropping a small amount of soil on the lowered coffin, two who hated him with everlasting venom, brought crushed glass already in soil, hoping it might seep through the coffin.

Margaret suffered the most when the matter of Harry's estate was raised. The big surprise was a serious slap in the face. The ever conniving Harry had written a new will. Typical, he told no-one and especially not his wife. His solicitor was under threat to not notify anyone until after his death and to delay that announcement for as long as possible.

It wasn't all sad news. Margaret was the main beneficiary but there were conditions all over the place. One legal eagle described it as a mine field will. Take a wrong step and kaboom.

His superannuation was only to be accessed once a month and then in limited withdrawal amounts. One half of his cash and shares were to be bequeathed to establish a trust for stray animals. What? Why? Margaret could only assume it was to reinforce the gong he never received but hoped would be granted posthumously.

You could see his thinking. He would receive his AO, pass away peacefully, and then be remembered by having the animal rescue centre named the *Harry Penshurst Animal Sanctuary*. But here Harry was his own worst enemy. By operating on such a secret footing, few if anyone knew of this good deed.

Margaret was never investigated for his death. There were enough persons of interest to keep both amateur and professional detectives busy.

The major change was her reluctance to re-join Probus. Not that she ever officially left but sitting at meetings when the overriding presence of her late husband hung around made it hard for the widow to engage.

Members tried to persuade her to return but what was now her holiday house in Portsea became more attractive. She got out of Brighton whenever she could and especially so when her former Probus club was meeting. Archie reckoned the Portsea back beach was far superior to the gentle waves at Brighton.

Margaret's brother was the last picked, the 23rd man in this game of death and delight. His life barely changed. He didn't discover a new extended family. He didn't meet a woman who could live in his battleground of woe. He lost his weed supplier but gained his freedom from those same people wanting to kill him. He stood still, made zero progress.

As for Harry's money, that became Terry's biggest loss. Promised a fee for helping his never-beloved brother-in-law to shuffle off this mortal coil, nothing happened. He tried arguing even begging his sister to splash the cash but she refused.

She did give him Harry's jewellery and that of course he wore with pride. No he didn't. Don't be silly. It was on sale in various pawn shops the day he got it.

Vale Henry.

Epilogue

The life of Henry Fitzgibbon Leigh Penshurst caused ripples. One could never describe the man as unremarkable. He was regarded as a diligent Probus president, a grower of fine red roses, an admirer of Airedale terriers, and a developer who had more misses than hits.

He was also pompous, self-obsessed, and conniving yet would never make the top 10 in the list of Ponzi scheme operators, and his passing was noted more for the people who wanted him dead than the good deeds he left behind.

Joan, his vice-president and replacement, slipped into the role with nary a skerrick of fuss, totally unlike her predecessor. Members loved Joan and she steered the club to new and exciting events. The membership of the Brighton Probus club continued to grow and soon it sported a burgeoning waiting list.

Three of its members started a new chapter in their senior years. Bobby[2] and sisters Patricia and Jean joined a new group they called PUDA—the Probus Unofficial Detective Agency. Their first case, as they called it, involved the murder of their Probus president. Not bad for starters. But was this a one off?

Mind you all three members were hardly lost for something to do in their retirement. As before, Probus was a serious consumer of their time although all three were busy elsewhere as well.

The retired police officer was his wife's carer as she battled Motor Neuron Disease, the horrible condition with no known cure—yet.

The sisters were now spending money on birthday cards and presents for members of their new but old families. Invitations to family events arrived consistently and their joy at discovering different generations of their kith and kin gave both women a new zest for living.

So the question arose. Is PUDA a one-off experience? Will it ever meet again? I mean, if they only deal with murders, how many homicides can one Probus club produce? Interesting question.

Watch this space.

Meet The Author

Hello. I write novels, plays and musicals and always enjoy hearing from readers.

You can read my play scripts online at www.foxplays.com.

My fiction and non-fiction books are at www.cenfoxbooks.com

I'll be most grateful if you take the time to leave a review on Amazon or Goodreads.

Amazon
https://www.amazon.com/s/ref=nb_sb_noss_1?url=search-alias%3Dstripbooks&field-keywords=cenarth+fox

Goodreads
https://www.goodreads.com/search?utf8=%E2%9C%93&q=Cenarth+Fox&search_type=books&search%5Bfield%5D=on
—

More Cenarth Fox Novels

Louise Beatrice Wellesley, nicknamed Plum because of her initials, is a brilliant, beautiful English actress studying at Cambridge in 1938. She's recruited as a spy for the Secret Service and is soon on stage in a Parisian nightclub wearing a costume to shock her mother. Sharing a dressing-room with Edith Piaf is never dull. War begins and in Paris, Louise fights Nazis, the French police, part of the Resistance, and a British traitor. Back home at Windsor Castle, she joins ENSA to star in Cinderella before the Royal Family. When the IRA kidnap a Royal, the leading lady conducts a Girls-own rescue and so impresses Winston, he demands she join the SOE. Dressed as a nun, Plum jumps out of plane near Lyon where she's tortured by the Gestapo, fights an archbishop, climbs the Pyrenees and, back in London, uncovers a mole in Baker Street thanks to someone who knows Sherlock Holmes. Go girl. How she returns to German-occupied Europe is amazing. How she escapes more so. She falls for an American and survives WW2 only to fight in another war. Will the world ever hear of her amazing secret life?

www.cenfoxbooks.com

Born in a London slum and sent on a hellish voyage
to a bloody war in Australia

A SWEEPING SAGA

broke, bullied, betrayed—but alive in
Van Diemen's Land

CENARTH FOX

Mr. Fox tells a marvellously researched tale of loss and redemption in the untamed bush of Van Diemen's Land. The descriptive detail and historical accuracy make A Sweeping Saga *a joy to read. This reader has even nominated it as required reading for my writers' group.* **Five stars** *A combination of fine scholarship and effective prose make A Sweeping Saga a great pleasure to read.*
Emeritus Professor Michael Roe University of Tasmania
I really enjoyed A Sweeping Saga and couldn't put it down. I was so disappointed when it was over. It must appeal universally.
Jonne Finnemore
That is a beautiful book cover. I'd buy your book just on the intriguing cover. **Michael Eisenhut. The Historical Fiction Club**

https://www.foxplays.com/novels/

From the author of
The Real Sherlock Holmes, Nursing Holmes, Sherlock Stock and Barrel,
and *The Schoolboy Sherlock Holmes*

SHERLOCK HOLMES
PLAYING THE GAME

CENARTH FOX

A delightfully imaginative pastiche. **Peter E Blau BSI**

An extraordinary book, one of the most enjoyable pieces of Holmesian fiction I've read in a long time ... a complex, ingenious and deliciously funny story of intersecting realities, and the conclusion is entirely satisfactory. I love it! **Roger Johnson**
Commissioning Editor: The Sherlock Holmes Journal

This book, a twist on Sherlock Holmes, is SO much fun! Mrs. Hudson has written a manuscript detailing all the errors in the Sherlock Holmes stories & she takes it to the editor of The Strand magazine, the original publisher of the stories. From there, it's a madcap romp of confusion for both the historical and the "fictional" characters until the final brilliant conclusion. **Goodreads 5 stars**

A completely different slant on Holmes and Watson...a grand tale.
Jean McCulloch Goodreads 4 stars